W9-AMO-923

A Treasured
Friendship

Miriam's Journal

A Fruitful Vine
A Winding Path
A Joyous Heart
A Treasured Friendship

Also by Carrie Bender

Whispering Brook Farm
Summerville Days

Carrie Bender

A Treasured Friendship

HERALD PRESS
Scottdale, Pennsylvania
Waterloo, Ontario

Library of Congress Cataloging-in-Publication Data
Bender, Carrie, date.
    A treasured friendship / Carrie Bender.
       p. cm. — (Miriam's journal ; 4)
    ISBN 0-8361-9033-5 (alk. paper)
    1. Married women—Pennsylvania—Fiction. 2. Farm life—
Pennsylvania—Fiction. 3. Amish—Pennsylvania—Fiction.
I. Title. II. Series: Bender, Carrie, date. Miriam's journal ; 4.
PS3552.E53845T74 1996
813'.54—dc20   95-47390
                                                CIP

The paper used in this publication is recycled and meets the minimum
requirements of American National Standard for Information
Sciences—Permanence of Paper for Printed Library Materials, ANSI
Z39.48-1984.

Scripture quotations and allusions imbedded in the text are based on
the *King James Version of the Holy Bible*, with some adaptation to
current English usage. For a list of Scripture references and other
credits, see pages 155-156.

A TREASURED FRIENDSHIP
Copyright © 1996 by Herald Press, Scottdale, Pa. 15683
    Published simultaneously in Canada by Herald Press,
    Waterloo, Ont. N2L 6H7. All rights reserved
Library of Congress Catalog Number: 95-47390
International Standard Book Number: 0-8361-9033-5
Printed in the United States of America
Cover art and inside line drawings by Joy Dunn Keenan
Book design by Paula M. Johnson
Series logo by Merrill R. Miller

05 04 03 02 01 00 99 98 97 96 10 9 8 7 6 5 4 3 2
15,000 copies in print

You never so touch
the ocean of God's love, as when you
forgive and love your enemies.

—Corrie Ten Boom

Contents

Estranged

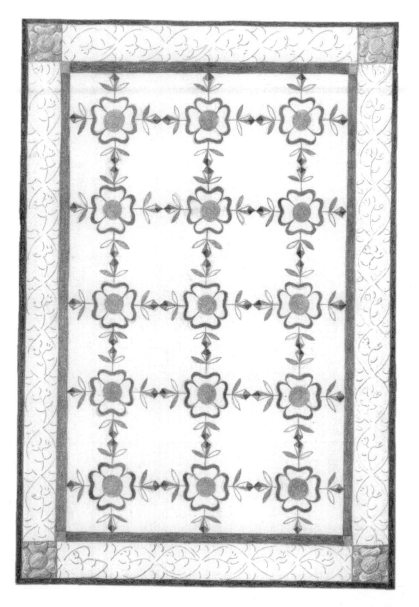

Surely springtime is the loveliest season. I'm sitting out here by the creek, drinking in the beauty. Mists hang over the meadow and the sun is beginning to thread its way through broken clouds. I love the early morning stillness when all is peaceful and quiet except for the chorus of robins and song sparrows, meadowlarks and other birds. Two baby squirrels are chasing each other up and down a tree trunk.

This is our alternate Sunday (when there are no church services). Something different seems to be in the atmosphere on a Sunday, something not present on weekdays: an almost sacred, holy, or hallowed feeling, compared to the everyday, humdrum routine. Maybe this is because we lay our work aside and reserve a day chiefly to worship God. There is a sweet benediction, an almost imperceptible something, that enriches the day. I found a poem that I like and want to copy in my journal:

Thankfulness for What You Could Not Afford

Suppose God charged us for the rain,
Or put a price on a songbird's strain
Of music, the dawn, mist on the plain.
How much would autumn landscapes cost,
Or a window etched with winter's frost,
And the rainbow's glory so quickly lost?

Suppose the people had to pay
To see the sunset's crimson play
And the magic stars on the Milky Way.
Suppose it was fifty cents a night
To watch the pale moon's silvery light,
Or watch a gull in graceful flight.

How much, I wonder, would it be worth
To smell the good, brown fragrant earth
In spring? The miracle of birth—
How much do you think people would pay
For a baby's laugh at the close of day?
Suppose God charged us for them, I say.

Suppose we paid to look at the hills,
For the rippling mountain hills,
Or the mating song of the whippoorwills,
Or the curving breakers of the sea,
For grace, and beauty, and majesty.
And all these things [God] gives us free.

—Missionary Messenger

Here comes little Crist to join me, just out of bed and still in his pajamas. He climbs on my lap, and I cuddle him close. Nate is singing in the barn, finishing his chores, with Peter's help. Dora and Sadie are having a tea party on an old tree stump nearby, setting their play dishes on it with their dolls sitting all around.

When I'm old and lonely, I'll look back with nostalgia and longing on these precious times when our little family is all together yet. So soon the time will come when all have flown the nest, so I'll enjoy them while I can.

Since it is Sunday and we have no church services, I'll also copy a few Bible verses. Titus 2, verses 11-14:

For the grace of God that brings salvation has appeared to all, teaching us that, denying ungodliness and worldly lusts, we should live soberly, righteously, and godly, in this present world; looking for that blessed hope, and the glorious appearing of the great God and our Savior Jesus Christ; who gave himself for us, that he might redeem us from all iniquity, and purify unto himself a peculiar people, zealous of good works. ≋

*T*oday was the last day of school, and I heaved a sigh of relief. Now we have our best helpers at home. Dora and Peter came trooping in the door, slamming their *Essekessel* (Pennsylvania German for lunch boxes) on the counter, and chanting:

> No more paper, no more books,
> No more teacher's crabby looks.
> No more blackboards, no more chalk,
> No more bossy teacher's talk.

"Now, now," I chided. "You know Teacher Ruth isn't bossy and crabby. She's a good teacher, and a very nice one, too."

"I know," Dora replied, "but guess what!" Her dark blue eyes flashed with importance in her heart-shaped face. "Ruth won't be our teacher next year. She's quitting. We'll have to find another teacher."

"*Ach* (oh) my, that spites me!" I sighed. "It'll be hard to find another teacher as good as Ruth. Are you sure it's really so?"

"Sure, it's true," Peter piped up as he hopped on the wood chest to hang his strawhat on a hook behind the stove. "Teacher Ruth wouldn't say a lie." His eyes sparkled in his freckled face as he opened his report card and said importantly, "I passed. I'll be going to second grade next year."

"Me too!" Dora chimed in. "I have mostly As and Bs, and only a few Cs. I'll be going to fourth grade."

"Next year I'll have a report card, too, won't I, *Mamm*

(Mom)?" six-year-old Sadie asked wistfully.

I assured her that she would, and the rest of the evening, off and on, I felt twinges of sadness. Our little family is growing up so fast. Soon little Crist will be the only one at home anymore. Then he, too, will be in school. Later, one by one, they'll be through school, and then soon of an age for *rumschpringing* (running around with the youth).

Time doesn't stand still, and neither would I want it to, but I'd like to capture the moments and the precious memories of their childhood and hold onto them. Yes, time flies. And every day we're a step closer to eternity and the hope of seeing Amanda again, our little daughter who has gone on before. It makes heaven seem closer and more like a reality to have a child who is with Jesus. ➢

June 17

*B*usy, happy June days. Strawberries, peas, haymaking, blooming roses, summer weather, fragrant honeysuckle vines. I love it all.

Tonight Nate and I actually went for a boat ride all by ourselves! It made me feel young and romantic again! I was taking the last jars out of the canner after a busy day of shelling and canning peas when Nate came in for a drink of water, hot and tired from making hay.

"Wouldn't it be nice if we could go for a boat ride tonight?" I remarked wistfully, as I brushed the *schtruwwlich* (unruly) hair back from my face and sank into a chair. "We haven't gone for ages, and it would be cool and peaceful by the water."

Nate merely shrugged his shoulders and mumbled a

noncommittal reply before going out to finish the chores. I felt a bit disillusioned and resentful as I washed the huge stack of supper dishes on the counter.

The children had helped well with the peas all day. As a reward I had given them permission to go for a pony ride as soon as the last peas were in jars. They gleefully piled into the cart, and fat little Merrylegs trotted out the lane pulling the cart.

I tried counting my blessings as I scrubbed pots and pans, but I still felt a bit disgruntled. Imagine my surprise when I saw Nate heading for the boat with the oars. Instantly my weariness left me, and I felt ashamed of my uncharitable thoughts. He's still the same dear, kind husband he always was!

The fragrant wild roses were blooming in profusion on the creek banks, the frogs were croaking melodiously, the air was sweet and cool, and everything felt just right, almost too good to be true. The lovely misty meadows, the tall stately trees, and the tranquil waters made me feel serene and peaceful. The twilight deepened, and one by one the fireflies appeared. It made me feel as if I'd been transported from the mundane things of life into the sublime.

"This is all so beautiful," I breathed. "How could heaven be any nicer?"

Nate didn't reply to that, but he had a question of his own. "Are you still glad you married me?"

He likes to ask me that every now and then. He knows the answer, but he likes to hear me say it! ⇛

We had our first meal of corn on the cob. They've come up with a super early kind, yet it's still delicious. Sadie has her two front teeth out and can hardly eat it, but she tries. She won't let me cut it off the cob for her.

Nate says Sadie's looking more like me every day—almost as chubby as I am. Oh my, I used to be slender, but not anymore. Maybe I should do something about it before it gets worse. But not while we have fresh sweet corn!

Nate and I made a trip to town today. On the way we were discussing the problem of not knowing where to look for a new teacher for fall. Nate was voted in as a board member at the last school meeting, and now it's partly our responsibility to find a teacher.

Not everyone has the talent to be a good teacher. Many of the girls capable of teaching choose instead to work in town for higher wages, or they marry young. We don't want to wait until the last minute to find a teacher, and school starts again in less than two months. Hopefully, one of the other board members will have found a prospect.

Traffic was heavy in town because of the tourists. We had to wait so long at a crossing that our horse got impatient and reared up on his hind legs. Oh dear, it's impossible to find a perfect horse. We thought this one was good but he has his faults, too.

If only the drivers of the cars would show a little mercy toward us. They drive so fast. I wish they'd slow down when they see that a horse is acting up. I guess they're too much in a hurry. All but the tourists—they do slow down.

Apparently they find us interesting.

I spent some time browsing through the secondhand shop and found an interesting-looking book for 25 cents. It's called *Wonderful Wife*, and I can hardly wait till I have time to read it. Not that I think I would ever be wonderful, but I might glean from it a few pointers on being a better wife. There's always room for improvement.

Our good neighbor Pamela Styer stopped in tonight and asked whether we'd made up our minds about being a host family for the German girl who prefers an Amish family. We promised to give her a definite answer within a week.

In some ways I think it would be interesting, but it might not be the best to have our family's faults exposed to an outsider like that. Maybe she is of the opinion that Amish families are perfect. I wonder if she is a Christian.

I hope we'll be given the wisdom to make the right decision, for much is at stake. We want to share our blessings with others and not just live for ourselves. So much has been given to us, and to whom much is given, much will be required. Is it selfish for us to wish just to be alone together as a family? ⊜

July 4

When Gloria Graham picked up milk this morning, she came into the house to chat for a few minutes. The first thing she said to me when she stepped through the door was "Oh my goodness, aren't you getting fat! I mean, I don't want to be nasty, but haven't you gained some weight lately?"

She said it perfectly guilelessly, but it annoyed me nevertheless. I wanted to retort, *I'm not as fat as you are, Gloria.* But just in time, I stopped myself. She can give a slam, but she can't take one. It's true, though, that she is slightly more than plump herself.

Gloria went on, "If I were you, I'd do something about it right away. I've found out that there's nothing harder than losing extra weight you've had for years and years. After awhile it gets to be impossible. I know that all too well."

She plopped down on the settee and eyed me critically. "I think I have just the thing for you, if you're willing to take it."

"But, but . . . I'm not that fat," I sputtered indignantly. I was kneading bread dough, and I boxed it extra hard.

"Now, now, don't get upset," Gloria said sweetly. "I'm just trying to do you a favor. You see, I'm selling vitamins and diet products, and I have just what you need. It's a powdered supplement to mix with water and drink before meals. It curbs your appetite and provides all the vitamins and minerals you need. Of course, you have to use it with my four-Cs diet to be effective."

"Four-seas diet?" I asked. "What's that?"

"Four Cs. You can only have four different kinds of food, and they all start with a C. It's so simple and easy to follow. You can have as much as you want of cottage cheese, carrots, celery, and cantaloupe."

"How about corn?" I wondered. "The sweet corn is ready in the garden, and I wouldn't want to miss that."

"Well, no, you can't have sweet corn. But when you're really motivated to lose weight, you don't mind doing without some foods. The best part about it is that you do lose weight."

I glanced at Gloria and wondered, *Why doesn't she practice what she preaches?* Her cheeks are fat, her arms are round and chubby, she's plump all over. Even her feet are fat, as you can see right through her sandals.

"I really think you should, Miriam," she continued in a cajoling tone. "Of course, you people don't have to worry about how you'll look in a bathing suit or shorts. But you'll feel wonderful!"

Wonderful! There's that word again.

I slapped the dough harder than necessary. "Suppose you and I start on the diet together. We could encourage each other and compare our weight losses."

Gloria was soon ready to leave after I said that. She mumbled something about having an ulcer and not being able to handle all that roughage.

"Think it over," she called back as she went out the door. "It really works, and it's fun and easy."

Hmmmmm! I wonder if Gloria really does have an ulcer, or if she just doesn't want to give up her ice cream and pastries and such.

After she left, I went upstairs and viewed myself with a critical eye in the full-length mirror inside the closet door. The only time I use that mirror is when I'm hemming up a new dress, to see if it's long enough. But now I studied my entire figure, and I came to the conclusion that Gloria is right.

I really do need to lose some weight (maybe fifteen or twenty pounds), but I'll wait until the sweet corn is over. Besides, the cantaloupes aren't ready yet. However, I won't use her expensive powdered drink, either. I'm still peeved at her for telling me I'm fat! ≫

*A*h, the sweet fragrance of summertime! In the early morning as I head for the barn, I take deep breaths of the fresh sweet air. My lungs are filled with the fragrance of dew-wet grasses, of new-mown hay, of early harvest apples ripening on the tree, and the heady aroma of corn growing in the fields after a nighttime shower, and the delightful scent of the sweet williams blooming by the gate.

I can't help but feel sorry for city dwellers. They have to gasp in the fumes of cars and trucks, and sometimes smog. Maybe they'd say the aroma of barns and animals and manure is air pollution. Oh well, each to their own opinion.

I hope I'll never take for granted the blessings of good health—to be able to be outside in the fresh invigorating air, to work hard, to be able to enjoy the beauties of nature. Why do we ever grumble about minor annoyances when we have the blessings of good health, and a heavenly Father to care for us?

On Wednesday evening Preacher Emanuel Yoder stopped in with the good news that they have found a teacher for our school. It's Pincher Joe's Franie. Grandpa Dave was here at the same time, and when he heard who was to be the new teacher, he nearly had a fit.

"One of Pincher Joe's daughters?" he exclaimed, in disbelief. "I think you're asking for trouble. She's bound to be a chip off the old block. Pincher was a real troublemaker in his younger days. He's always been a real penny-pincher and drives a hard bargain. I've heard it said about him that if you could buy him for what he's worth, and sell him again for what he thinks he's worth, you'd strike it rich."

"Now, Dave, who are we to judge?" Emanuel chided mildly. "She was willing to take the job when we asked her, and we'll give her a fair trial. We're hoping for the best, and we're relieved that we've found someone.

"Now I have a question for you," he said, turning to Nate and me. "The teacher has to have a place to board that's close to the school. Would you be able to board her? Think it over, and let me know by the weekend."

We did talk it over. When Pamela Styer came for her answer about the German girl, we told her we felt it would be our duty to board the new teacher instead. She agreed, but asked us to keep it in mind for later.

So, we're glad that our search for a teacher is over. We hope she's got what it takes. I expect she'll like it here and will be able to make herself at home. I don't know her well, but from what I've seen of her, she seems like a nice girl. ⧉

July 11

One by one, the shelves in the cellar are filling up. First it was rhubarb, then strawberries, peas, cherries, string beans, pickles, and soon we'll be canning applesauce from the early apples.

Dora and Sadie are good helpers. Even little Crist willingly trots up and down the steps, bringing up empty jars as we need them, and carrying cooled cans of applesauce down to the cellar, one at a time, carefully!

Yesterday Dora announced that we already have over a thousand quarts of canned goods. We will also freeze some things. Frozen food tastes better than the canned, and it's less work to put up the food. But we use the locker in town, and that's not as handy as a freezer at home.

Peter is outside with Dad these days, from sunup to sundown, coming in only for meals. He's a real farmer boy. These are busy, happy days—the children are out of the demanding toddler stage and learning to work.

Tonight after the children were in bed, I was waiting for Nate to come in. I stood at the open bedroom window, breathing in the refreshing evening air and absorbing some of the quietness of the night. My thoughts turned to a book that Priscilla loaned me called *Now Is the Time to Love*. I'll copy some of it here, to remind Nate and me.

Now is the time to love. Tomorrow is too late to rock the baby. Tomorrow the toddler won't be asking questions. Tomorrow the schoolboy will not need help with his lessons. Nor will he bring home his school and neighborhood friends to share in family fun. Tomorrow the teenager will have made his major decisions and will not feel a need for the nearness he longs for and which we can give him now. And tomorrow our child will be close to us or a stranger to us depending upon how we use our time for him now.

—*John M. Drescher*

The time before our children are grown and gone is so short. There is teaching, guiding, instructing, warning, and nurturing and loving to do. It seems like such an awesome task. Upon parents rests the greatest responsibility in the world, the job of molding lives and shaping character. "The hand that rocks the cradle is the hand that rules the world" (William Ross Wallace). And the most important thing is to be a good example. ≷

Our no-church Sunday. We're having an all-day rain, so we stayed home all day. Finally I got a chance to read my *Wonderful Wife* book. I felt a little guilty about reading it on a Sunday. I reasoned that if it helps me to be a better wife it should be all right.

Mostly I just skimmed over the book, but I was really impressed. It makes it sound like you can change your marriage from a mediocre one to, well, a heavenly one, by following the guidelines in the book. The difference between the two kinds of marriage is like the contrast between weeds and flowers, or between crumbs on the floor and a rich banquet on the table!

Hmmm! I can't wait to try out some of these things on Nate! He's a good husband, but I just wonder what he'll do when I start admiring him and praising him for his manly qualities, like it says. The book makes it sound as though every man has a craving to hear appreciation for his manly actions. If this is missing, he becomes "hardened" as he learns to do without it. When he has to repress this wish for admiration, he can't blossom in love.

Well, well, you're never too old to learn something new. Just wait till the next opportunity I have to make Nate feel like a real manly man! I'll want to be careful, though, to make sure it's sincere, not just flattery. He'd be sure to detect a phony compliment right away. ≥

Gloria Graham was here again, and my, she's a high pressure saleslady. She had a bottle of her Miracle Diet Powder along and praised it to the skies. Gloria said a lot of other women are using it, and how wonderful it makes you feel, young and energetic, and more bounce to the ounce. The diet is so simple, she says, no weighing or measuring of foods, and no counting calories. You can have all you want of those four foods.

I felt myself weakening. Just this morning Nate had read a little verse aloud from the weekly paper:

> He couldn't say no to whipped-cream pie
> And for that reason he here doth lie.

Underneath was a picture of a mound and a gravestone, and this question: "Are you guilty of digging your grave with your teeth?"

Hmmmm! Maybe it would be good for me to go on a diet. Didn't it say in the *Wonderful Wife* book that a woman could have more fresh, radiant health if she'd eat mostly natural, wholesome foods such as fresh vegetables and fruits? Finally I agreed to try the diet but said I wouldn't take the diet powder. Wow! that didn't suit Gloria at all. She wants to sell her diet powder, that's what!

"Try it," she urged. "I'm leaving a bottle here for you, and if it isn't everything I say it is, it won't cost you a cent. How's that for an offer? And do try to walk two miles a day. It'll help you lose weight more efficiently."

"Two miles!" I gasped. "Where would I go, and how would I find the time?"

"Just walk briskly out the road for a mile and back again," she replied confidently. "It shouldn't take long." She set the bottle of Miracle Diet Powder on the counter and breezed happily out the door.

Well then, I guess I have no more excuses. The first two batches of sweet corn are over, and I've had my fill of corn on the cob for this summer.

The cantaloupes are ripe, the early celery stalks are big enough to cut, and we have a nice row of carrots in the garden. Tonight I saved three gallons of milk from the evening milking and set it out to sour for making cottage cheese. As soon as it's ready, I'll have my four Cs and can go on the diet.

However, I won't take the diet powder. I don't believe in taking vitamins when we have so many fresh vegetables in the garden. ≫

July 24

*T*he girls need white *Schatzlin* (little aprons) before Sunday, and I want to make a white *Kapp* (prayer covering) for myself. The afternoons these days are too oppressively warm to venture outside, so I'll wait for cooler evening air to do my outside work.

This afternoon I'll sit at the sewing machine, if the pesky *Micke* (flies) don't bother me too much. I've heard say that in the cities there aren't many flies, and people can open windows without putting in screens. That's hard to believe—so different from here on the farm.

Yesterday I read a few snatches again in *Wonderful Wife* and learned that women are supposed to wear frilly, light-colored dresses to show the feminine contrast to men's coarse dark-colored clothes.

Well, that's certainly out for Amish women. Plain and dark dresses and aprons are in the *Ordnung* (church rules). To have a halo of fluffy hair surrounding the face wouldn't be allowed, either. Amish women's hair should be pulled back from the face so tightly and severely that it lifts the eyelids slightly, or so it seems. (I hope this doesn't sound rebellious.)

Now a report on giving praise to the male in my life. On Monday when Nate came in for dinner, I finally gathered up enough courage to make a stab at it. "You know," I said, trying to sound casual, "your beard really makes you look manly. It becomes you so well."

Nate simply stared at me for a long moment, and I was flustered enough to blush. "I—I mean," I stammered, "it makes you look like a real man."

"Isn't that what I am?" he asked, with a bewildered look on his face.

"Of course," I quickly replied. "But—I—er—ah. . . ."

The children came running in to the table then, and I was saved from further explanation. I sure goofed that one!

Then on Tuesday, I gave it another try. When Nate lifted a heavy milk can into the cooler, I said, "Wow, you've really got big muscles. You certainly are well built."

Nate gave me another strange look, then he grinned. That was a little better. I'll have to think of something else to admire him for today. I wonder how soon I can expect our marriage to become heavenly. ≋

Dora's patch of pumpkin crush marigolds out along the fence is as pretty as a picture. She's been watering and weeding them, and I believe maybe she talks to them, too.

Sadie claims a little round bed of pink-and-white impatiens for her own, and I often see her sitting by it with her doll. Nate says it just matches her, round and sweet, and Dora's flower bed fits her, pretty and eye-catching.

Well, I think I'm finally motivated myself now to try Gloria's diet, instead of just doing it to please her. Several embarrassing things happened yesterday, and now I'm ready.

In the morning Peter and I were feeding the chickens. Just as I stepped into the pen with a bucket of mash to pour into the hopper, Peter's beloved little pet chick, Bo-Peep, ran under my foot, and I stepped on him. There was a sickening crunch. The anguish and horror in Peter's eyes were almost more than I could bear.

"Mamm," he cried reproachfully. "Why are you so *fett und dappich* (fat and clumsy)?" He sobbed like a baby, and I could have cried, too. I felt like an elephant or something of similar proportions.

Then in the evening we hitched up to go and visit Priscilla and Henry. When we drove up to the tie railing, Henry came out from the shop, smiling congenially, and Priscilla and Miriam Joy came out of the house to welcome us.

I hurried out of the carriage and rather forcibly stepped on the carriage step. With a sharp crack, it broke off. The next thing I knew, I was sprawled on the ground. Nothing was hurt but my pride.

Little Crist sprang to my side and tried to help me up. He said reprovingly, "Next time don't be so *schusslich* (careless), Mamm."

By this time the others were trying hard not to laugh. I was so embarrassed that then and there I resolved to slim down. The cottage cheese is ready, and tomorrow morning at five o'clock I'm starting.

Since my body is a spoiled brat, I'm going to give it some strict rules. No more can it have whatever it wants whenever it wants it. After all, eating is fleeting, fasting is lasting. *Self-discipline!* here I come. ⧽

July 31

I had nearly forgotten about walking two miles a day. Then tonight Gloria breezed in the door and called cheerily, "How goes the sailing on the four seas?"

I told her it was "good, so far," and she said, "Grab your bonnet and hop into my car. I'll take you along to the gym for a calorie-burning workout."

It took me about ten minutes to convince her that that wouldn't be necessary. She can really be insistent. I promised her I'd take a long walk back in our meadow. Finally she agreed that would be okay, as long as it's a fast, brisk walk, not just a stroll to enjoy the scenery.

So, after she left, I started out the cow lane at a brisk trot, chuckling to myself about how it would look to others to see an Amish woman doing push-ups and sit-ups in a gymnasium. Probably someone would've snapped a picture and put it on the front page of the daily paper with a big headline: **Local Amish Woman Working Out to Win the Battle of the Bulge!**

I didn't even want to be seen walking for exercise. What would the neighbors think? That's why I went out the cow lane instead of out on the road. I was huffing and puffing and walking so briskly that I was half running when I heard a rattling sound behind me. I whirled around, and there was neighbor Eli, pushing along on his scooter, with a concerned and worried look on his face.

"What's wrong?" he asked. "Is someone hurt? Are you looking for Nate?"

Then it dawned on me. Eli had seen me trotting like that, and I looked so undignified that he thought it surely must be an emergency. So he followed me on the scooter to see if he could help.

How could I explain without seeming utterly ridiculous? I managed to mumble a few words of explanation, and he hightailed it out the lane faster than he came in. I walked back to the house, sedately and demurely. I wouldn't disgrace myself again. *Dumb me!* I hadn't thought about how the cow lane back through the meadow can be plainly seen from the road.

I walked back to the house leisurely. The peaceful twilight twitter of the birds soothed my spirits, and the refreshing breeze cooled my hot cheeks. Doesn't it say somewhere in Timothy that "bodily exercise profits little"?

That evening I decided that running a household, doing chores, gardening, and lawn mowing would be enough exercise for me. After all, I don't sit and watch TV for hours at a time like Gloria does. So much for that! ⪼

The children are counting the days until Teacher Franie comes to board with us. I too am counting the days I have left before she comes, but for a slightly different reason. It's not that I don't look forward to her coming, but somehow I think life is more relaxing when it's just our family. No doubt she'll fit right in and soon will seem like one of us.

Today I thought up another manly compliment for Nate. He was throwing huge forkfuls of manure onto the spreader. As I passed with a bucket of slop for the pigs, I called, "Wow, your muscles really bulge when you do that. I can see them ripple underneath your shirtsleeves."

I don't know how he took that one. He gave me a long look as though he was trying to figure me out and wasn't able to.

Slightly embarrassed, I hurried on. I wonder what results I'm supposed to see, and how soon. Somehow, I'm afraid it doesn't seem quite natural to him. What am I doing wrong? Maybe I should just concentrate on improving myself—having a worthy character, moral courage (such as sticking to a diet), self-dignity, and being an all-around good Christian. ≋

Woe is me! I'm off my diet and feel hopeless and powerless to get back on again. I've lost all desire. The first day I was on it was wonderful. The cottage cheese was delicious, eaten with chopped celery and shredded carrots. I put several cantaloupes into the spring in the cellar to get nice and cold. When I came in from hoeing the garden, hot and thirsty, I thought I'd never before tasted anything quite so delicious.

The next day I didn't feel hungry for cottage cheese again, but I disciplined myself to eat it anyway. By the third day, I was tired of it all—all the four Cs. But I denied myself and ate a little bit of everything allowed. The fourth day I was very hungry, but not for cottage cheese and cantaloupe!

I barely survived the fifth and sixth day. Then last evening the hunger pangs hit me in earnest. I wanted what I couldn't have, and I felt deprived and irritable. I felt peeved at Gloria for coercing me into the diet, and peeved at myself for falling for it.

After the chores were finished, two carriages drove in the lane. What a surprise! Priscilla, Henry, and Miriam Joy breezed into the kitchen, carrying pizzas, ready to bake, and Barbianne and Rudy brought a freezer full of hand-cranked, homemade ice cream.

We were all so glad to see them. Soon the kitchen was filled with the wonderful aroma of homemade pizzas baking. I felt hungrier than I ever was before in my life, and my willpower was fast disappearing.

At first I fought temptation, but by the time Priscilla took the pizza out of the oven, I had made my decision. So much for Gloria's old fad diet. It was entirely unbalanced anyway. No meat, no milk, no variety. Why did I ever let her brainwash me like that?

The pizza was scrumptious! I enjoyed every bite of it. The vanilla ice cream topped with chocolate sauce was the best I'd ever tasted.

We sat and visited awhile, then, sure enough—Grandpa Daves must have smelled the pizza. Their trusty old steed came plodding in the lane, and we then had a party—a real old-fashioned gabfest.

Dave's stories had everyone laughing. He had picked up one from the newspaper. A camera-toting tourist asked some Amishmen to hold still so she could snap their pictures, but they ignored her and went on baling hay. The tourist assumed that the Amish were paid to look quaint and play their roles for the visitors. So she complained to the local chamber of commerce about this.

What a joke! Don't the tourists realize that we're real people, not here just to put on a show for them? Anyhow, we don't like to pose for photos because that is making an image, breaking one of the Ten Commandments.

Grandma Annie brought us up-to-date on all the community news, telling us who had a baby, who broke a leg, and whose cow had twins. It was a most enjoyable evening. But, oh dear, it wonders me what Gloria will say next time she comes. I hope she won't be too mad! ⇛

August 8

I feel disquieted within to-night, unhappy and troubled. I don't like to lose one of my friends, no matter what her faults. Most people would've thought, *Good-bye and good riddance,* but that's not me.

Gloria came for milk tonight. When I saw her, I felt like hiding in the cellar or the springhouse. At the last minute I decided to stay and get it over with. I knew I'd have to face her sooner or later.

When Gloria came into the kitchen, cheerily enough, she cried, "My, you look great! I can see you've lost weight! How did it go?"

I hemmed and hawed and finally just lamely said, "I— I've gone off the diet and don't plan to go back on."

"What!" she howled, stamping her foot. "Don't say that! Sure you'll go back on. I have another can of Miracle Diet Powder along for you. Don't give up so easily!"

The *Schpeck* (fat) on her leg quivered. Was she really that angry or just pretending, to scare me into using her powder?

I shook my head. "I've decided to keep on eating a balanced diet—just like I've been doing, only cutting back on desserts and baked goods. I think I'll be able to do better that way."

I tried to say it calmly and evenly, but Gloria was visibly upset. She gave me a defiant look and asked, with a note of belligerence in her voice, "But didn't you just love the diet powder?"

"No, I didn't take it," I admitted, feeling like I was a naughty little girl being reprimanded by her teacher. "I didn't think it was necessary."

Gloria stamped her foot again and the *Schpeck* on her leg quivered all the more. "For heaven's sake, why didn't you follow my instructions?"

Sadie came running to me and hid her face in my skirt. Poor little thing! She knew something was wrong. I did my best to explain nicely to Gloria, but she left in a huff, mumbling something about "these dumb Dutchmen." Even her car sounded angry as she tore out the lane amid flying gravel.

Oh dear, what have I done? Maybe I'm just too dumb,

but I've made up my mind not to be brainwashed again. I opened the Bible for guidance. Was it just by chance? The first thing I read was what Paul wrote to the Corinthians: "Wherefore, if meat make my brother to offend, I will eat no flesh while the world stands, lest I make my brother to offend." I felt all the more guilty.

Should I go to the phone shanty and call Gloria and tell her I'm sorry I offended her? Shall I agree to eat exactly the way she wants me to, and take her powder besides? I decided to put a check in the mail for her, for the can of powder that was still here, and write a nice little note to try to smooth things over.

Little Crist climbed on my lap with his horsie book for me to tell him a story, and soon I felt better. At least someone still loves me and needs me. But I still feel wounded and disquieted within. I can hardly stand it when someone's mad at me.

I can hardly believe that Gloria's really so angry over such a little matter. At first I thought it was only a joke and that she's pretending to be mad. But I soon found out it's real. How can she be so unreasonable? ⇒

August 22

No matter how hard I try, I'm never so well organized that I do all my sewing in winter. If I did, I wouldn't have to sew a stitch during the busy summer months. This week wasn't quite so busy, and Nate needed a pair of *Latzhosse* (broadfall pants). So I got out my sewing machine and happily made him a pair.

While he was fitting them on, I decided to rack my brain

for a manly compliment for him. I couldn't think of a thing on the spur of the moment. Finally I blurted out, in English, "Wow, you sure look swell!" I had heard Gloria say that to her cat one time.

Nate gave me a strange look. "I do believe it's good that Gloria Graham is mad at you. You're picking up some of her *englisch* (non-Amish) ways. Since when isn't speaking Dutch good enough for us?"

He said it kindly, but I felt reprimanded. My compliments aren't doing a bit of good! I feel tired and discouraged tonight, almost like crawling into a hiding place for a few weeks and peeking out every now and then to see if it's safe to come out and dwell among people again.

If only Gloria would stop in and be her old jolly self again. That would take a burden off my back. We met her in her car as we were driving to town on Tuesday. I waved to her, but she looked the other way. I did send her a check for the diet powder, along with a nice little note. A few days later it was back in the mailbox with "Refused, Return to Sender" written on it. She didn't even open it.

Well, maybe Nate's right. Perhaps it will turn out for good in the long run. It's not the first time she's been mad at us. Once she even threatened to sue us, and later she was sweet as honey and her words as smooth as butter again. Hopefully this won't mean much either. ✐

August 29

*T*eacher Franie is here. School starts on Monday, and her dad brought her over in the trottin' buggy tonight. Dora showed her to her room.

As I passed her doorway when I was putting away laundry, I heard her say, "Oh, I'm so disappointed. I wanted a room facing west." I felt taken aback, and I hurried down the stairs instead of going into her room for a friendly chat with her.

All evening I found myself mentally comparing her unfavorably with Barbianne, our *Maut* (hired girl) when Crist was a baby. But then I remembered that Barbianne had her faults, too, when she first came, and soon we all loved her.

"Franie has a way of eyeing things critically, or maybe it just seems so to me. She has a disapproving stare," I said to Nate tonight as we were preparing for bed. "It just rattles me."

He asked me, "Are you sure you're really welcoming her? Or are you resenting her as an intruder in our family?"

I was cut to the quick, and my feelings were hurt. But I determined to do some soul-searching, to shape up my attitudes, with God's help. I am determined I will love her and accept her, no matter what. ⇨

September 2

What makes some people so much harder to love than others? I suppose it's their ways, their little mannerisms, whether they're tactful or blunt, kind or selfish, friendly or curt, touchy or not easily offended.

I've been trying to figure out Franie and find it nearly impossible. One moment she can be open and friendly; the next she'll be reserved and withdrawn. I wonder what causes these abrupt changes of mood. Maybe she has a hard time adjusting to our busy family.

School days are here again! It seems like just a few weeks ago that summer vacation began. Now little Sadie is a scholar, too, in the first grade.

The first week they only have half days of school. Sadie comes home with glowing eyes and lots of stories to tell. It's obvious that she loves it, and Dora and Peter are enthused about school, too. I just hope it stays that way! ≫

October 3

*G*loria Graham stopped in again tonight. Her hair was piled up on top of her head in a new fashion, and she wore white, knee-high boots. Her lips were painted bright red. She smiled patronizingly, patted little Crist on the head, walked over to me, and said sweetly and demurely, "Here's a little note I wish you would read."

The jewels on her ring sparkled as she handed me the note. Suddenly I remembered that I hadn't seen her husband, George, for awhile. What happened to him? Did he leave her even though she gave up her gorgeous Persian cat for his sake?

I was almost afraid to open her "little note." But then I was buoyed by the thought that maybe she wanted to say she's sorry for the way she's been acting. I hoped she was asking for forgiveness and wanting to be friends again. Slowly I unfolded the sheet and began to read. It surely wasn't what I was expecting!

Just a Little Rhyme

Tobacco is a filthy weed.
It was the devil who sowed the seed.
It picks your pockets, spoils your clothes,
And makes a chimney out of your nose.

—Unknown

Of all things! What in the world brought this on? I stood there, puzzled, not knowing what to make of it. Gloria watched me closely to see my reaction, with a sort of triumphant, cat-got-the-mouse look on her face.

"Aha!" she said craftily. "What do you say to that? Is it true?"

I didn't answer right away, and she took a step closer. "Well, is it?"

I took a step backward, and she followed. The screen door slammed, and I saw little Crist running to the barn. I wished I could do the same. Her perfume was strong and her presence overbearing.

Finally I regained my composure and found my voice. "Sure, smoking and chewing is a bad habit." I tried to sound natural, but found my voice quivering. "But there are some good uses for tobacco. We use it to dust the potato plants. It kills the bugs," I added lamely.

Then I remembered a recent article I had read. "Anyhow, the newspaper says that they are going to make tobacco produce drugs and medicine to help sick people. But why do you bring this up? You know neither Nate nor I use tobacco for smoking or chewing."

"Why!" she said icily. "You should ask! You know why! You people think you're so good, and yet you raise tobacco. You're helping other people become slaves to it." She spat out the words, then turned on her heels and stalked out.

At the door she turned and added, "And yet you're too good to use my diet products."

I've been sighing wearily ever since she left. Being on the outs with someone wears me to a frazzle. I wonder why she said "you think you're so good." I know I'm not good, and Jesus says there is none good but God. We're not putting out any tobacco next year. Nate just decided that last week. But it's not because of what Gloria said.

All this has made me think, though. If no one farmed tobacco, no one could become a slave to the noxious weed. No wonder Gloria was indignant! Oh dear, life sure seems complicated sometimes. ⋙

October 7

*T*eacher Franie is with us at the breakfast and supper table, but she packs her lunch for at school. A few days ago, Nate said to me, "Did you notice that when we bow our heads to say thanks at the table, she keeps her head bowed a lot longer than the rest of us?"

I had noticed, and it bothers me. Nate is the head of the home and at the head of the table. He's the one to indicate when we start and finish. It almost makes me feel like we are heathens and she is a saint, if she prays so much longer. It's uncomfortable for us, not daring to move or start eating until she finally raises her head.

Nate then decided that we'll all bow our heads and pray longer if that's the way she's been used to doing it. At the breakfast table the next morning, we all bowed our heads a long time—all was so quiet the clock could be heard ticking. Little Crist was fidgeting, and finally I peeked. Nate raised his head then, and I thought surely that was long enough for Franie, but lo and behold, she still kept her head bowed almost a minute longer than the rest of us!

When breakfast was eaten and we again bowed our heads to return thanks, the same thing happened. Since then, we've discovered that no matter how long we pray, she prays several minutes longer. Somehow, I'm no longer impressed. It seems to me that she does it for attention or to make a show of her spirituality. But maybe I'm being judgmental. ⮐

October 24

*B*eautiful fall weather. The nights are cool and crisp, and at night the hoots of the screech owl can be heard from the trees along the creek. A sweater feels good while raking leaves, and there's a certain tang in the air. Wild geese are honking and winging their way southward.

I'm reminded of a poem we read in school.

October's Bright Blue Weather

O suns and skies and clouds of June,
And flowers of June together,
Ye cannot rival for one hour
October's bright blue weather.

42

When loud the bumblebee makes haste
Belated thriftiness vagrant,
And goldenrod is dying fast,
And lanes with grapes are fragrant;

When gentians roll their fringes tight
To save them from the morning,
And chestnuts fall from satin burrs
Without a sound of warning.

When on the ground red apples lie
In piles like jewels shining,
And redder still on old stone walls
Are leaves of woodbine twining;

When all these lovely wayside things
Their white-winged seeds are sowing,
And in the fields still green and fair,
Late aftermaths are growing.

When springs run low and on the brooks
In idle golden freighting,
Bright leaves sink noiseless in the hush
Of woods for winter waiting.

O suns and skies and flowers of June,
Count all you boast together,
Love loveth best of all the year,
October's bright blue weather.

—*Helen Hunt Jackson*

The children seem to like school and their new teacher, and for that I am so thankful. Nate is at a school board meeting tonight. We're hoping everything will continue to go smoothly and peaceably. At least I hope there are no problems. Whenever I ask Franie how things are going, she just shrugs her shoulders. Is that her way of saying everything's all right? ≽

October 31

*T*he leaves on the trees are wondrously golden and colorful these days, and the air is sharp and cool. That adds a spring to the step. Soon the winds and the rain will bring all the leaves down. So I'll appreciate it while I can.

It's trick-or-treat time again among the *Englischer*. There are some pranksters in the neighborhood. This morning all of us along this road found that our mailboxes were smashed sometime during the night. Now wouldn't that be great fun, going around doing that? Broken pumpkins were littered around, too, and a corn shock was dragged into the middle of the road.

This afternoon Nate went to a sale with neighbor Eli, in Eli's trottin' buggy. Just west of town a car passed, and *Wham!* something hit Nate on the chin. Egg yolk dribbled down into his beard and under his collar. *Ugh!*

Nate said that although the Bible tells us, "Love your enemies," at that moment he could've cheerfully grabbed the egg thrower and boxed his ears.

Eli nearly fell off his seat laughing at the comical sight of egg dripping off Nate. He even said that if enough people buy eggs to throw, it should boost the egg price, which would be to his benefit since he has laying hens.

Well! I guess he wouldn't have laughed if he would've been hit!

Tonight after the children were in bed, I played a trick on Nate. I really don't know what got into me. I'm ashamed of myself now, but, anyway, we got a good laugh out of it.

I was sorting through a bag of old clothing I'd gotten at the outgrown shop, to cut into strips for rugmaking—things like skirts, blouses, slacks, and dresses that *englisch* people wear. When I came across an old curly-haired wig at the bottom of the bag, I went into the bedroom and fitted it on. I couldn't believe how different I looked—I hardly knew myself.

On a sudden impulse, I also put on a long gown that completely covered my own dress. Then I sneaked out the front door, came around to the kitchen door, and knocked. Nate was sitting at the table reading. When he came to the door, I stood in the shadows and said, in a disguised voice, "Could you help me start my car, please?"

I hoped I'd be able to keep a straight face. It was so funny to hear him say in his Sunday-best manners, "I don't know much about cars, but I'll try to help." He got a flashlight and started to walk with me out the lane.

Suddenly I stepped close to him, laid my hand on his arm, and cooed, "Oh, you're so handsome!"

Nate jerked back, really startled, and made a beeline for the house. I was laughing so hard that I could hardly run. But I managed to slip under the trees to the front door, went through the hall, and met him at the bedroom door.

Oh, it was *soooo* funny, seeing the flabbergasted look on his face. He was probably wondering how this *englisch* woman got into the house so fast. Not till I took off the wig did he recognize me, and then we laughed until the tears flowed. For a while, I thought I couldn't stop my fit of laughing.

Now I'm a sane, decent, sensible woman again. I guess it doesn't hurt to have a good laugh once in a while, but I don't think I'll ever do anything like that again. I'm too old to be so silly. I hope my grandchildren won't ever find this out. What would they think? ⧽

November 11

*H*enry was here this morning with some good news! They have a little daughter, and he said she's healthy, as far as they know, and Priscilla is fine.

"She looks just like me," he said, a bit proudly, "and her name is Bathsheba."

Bathsheba! Of all the pretty names there are to choose, and they took that one. It isn't really an Amish name, although I've heard there are a few Amish women with that name in other states. I hope the dismay didn't show on my face. I think I expressed appropriate congratulations, though.

When I think of Bathsheba in the Bible, I think of an adulteress. She must've been beautiful and desirable. Actually, David was worse than she was in that he misused his position as king. In spite of this, he was a man after God's own heart, for he worshiped the Lord, strove after righteousness, and repented of his sins.

I can hardly wait to see the new baby. Dora is all excited about it, too. She wants to spend her evenings and weekends there if possible. ⊚

November 14

*T*his morning we had planned to go see baby Bathsheba. However, when we woke up, we were greeted by the first snowfall of the season! The children hailed it with cries of delight and eagerly got dressed. The roads were slightly hazardous, but since it was Saturday and the children had no school, we decided to go anyway.

We got out our overshoes and heavy coats and shawls and the good warm buggy robes. Then we piled into the carriage and rode along, happily singing all the frosty-snowy songs we could remember. Our good old horse danced and pranced, and the carriage wheels squeaked and squealed in the frozen snow. But it was warm and cozy under the blankets.

I had a few anxious moments, though. While going down the hill past Grandpa Dave's house, we slid into the ditch. The brakes were useless, and I clutched little Crist so hard that he hollered, "*Loss mich geh* (let me go)!" But Nate is a good driver, and we slipped and slid safely down the hill. Soon we arrived at Henry and Priscilla's without mishap.

What a beautiful baby for such a name! I know I shouldn't feel that way. Henrietta would be a more appropriate name, though not an Amish name either; she does look a lot like Henry.

Priscilla said that Henry wants to give all their children biblical names. I certainly like that idea, but it's too late for us now. Peter is the only one of our family (besides Nate and me) who has a biblical name. Oh well, as long as they turn out to be good Christians . . . ⪧

November 19

I've been reading some more in the *Wonderful Wife* book. It greatly amused me to read the chapter about childlike sauciness. I can't imagine me ever trying anything like that on Nate!

According to the author, when a husband mistreats, ignores, insults, or criticizes his wife, she is to respond with pretend anger and ham it up. She could stamp her foot and say things like, "Oh, you hard-hearted thing, is this the way you treat your poor little wife who slaves for you all day? Why should I bother talking to you any more?"

Then she can swish saucily out of the room. But it's supposed to be mostly a game, acting like a child with spunk and sauciness. A tear or two, quivering lips, and a pout are supposed to arouse a feeling of tenderness in a man and attract him.

The offended wife can open her eyes wide, raise her chin, swish out of the room, and slam the door behind her. It's supposed to be a cute and adorable way of showing childlike spunk and softening your husband. Hmmm. . . . I'll have to keep that in mind!

Just joking! I can't imagine me ever treating kindhearted Nate that way. Besides, it sounds more like what a spoiled brat would do, rather than a Christian woman.

I came across a small verse the other day that seemed to me to be the epitome of marital oneness. It sure is something to strive for, at any rate.

> They were so truly one,
> That no one knew which ruled,
>   and which obeyed.
> He ruled because she would obey,
>   and she by loving ruled the most.

—Unknown

It couldn't get any better than that, could it?

Priscilla once told me, before she and Henry were married, that he gave her an interesting but sad little article to read. It was the story of a selfish, headstrong married couple. Each wanted their own way.

If the husband wanted to watch TV and the wife wanted the TV off, they had a big fight. If he wanted a home-cooked meal and she wanted to go out to eat, another fierce battle erupted. Each time they had a disagreement, there were angry words and hard feelings.

One evening when he came home from work, she had rearranged the furniture. He didn't like the change, so he moved it all back where it had been. She was furious! As soon as he left for work the next morning, she again rearranged the furniture to suit herself. That evening when he came home and saw what she had done, he angrily moved it all back.

This went on for several more days, until the wife left and filed for divorce. Neither gave in to the other, neither went the second mile (not even halfway), and each lived only to please oneself.

Henry told Priscilla that after she marries him, she could arrange her furniture exactly the way she wants, do whatever she wants, and have whatever she wants. She pledged the same to Henry.

That was a nice and loving thing to say, but I'm sure they both forgot it during the time they were out of sync with each other. I'm so glad they learned to give up their self-will and live peaceably and harmoniously, in a community where love can grow and flourish. ⪼

November 21

*Y*esterday was our ex-teacher Ruth's wedding, and we were all invited. School was closed to let her former pupils attend, and teacher Franie came too. It was a beautiful, clear, and crisp day, just right for a wedding.

Isaac and Rosemary were there from Minnesota, and their whole family was along. How the children have grown, especially Matthew! And Rosemary is as sweet and gracious as ever. Isaac had the *Aafang* (beginning sermon) in the wedding service, and it was good to hear him preach again.

They say their little settlement in Minnesota is thriving and doing well. They're glad they moved out there and wouldn't want to move back. Now they think everything is so crowded around here. There's so much traffic that they're almost scared to drive through town.

The wedding feast was delicious, and no one had any suspicion that something was tainted. But after we were home, at around midnight, we all started to have terrible stomach pains. There was a lot of running down the steps to the bathroom and groaning on the way back to bed. Today we're all feeling weak and tired but much better than last night.

Tonight when Nate went to Eli's to borrow a scythe, he found out that almost all the wedding guests were likewise afflicted. Some say it was the homemade cheese, and others blame the gravy. It reminds me of the time Nate had food poisoning—at least this wasn't as serious as that. All's well that ends well! ≫

November 26

Sadie and I walked over to Grandpa Dave's tonight. A full moon was rising in the east, and the air smelled fresh and woodsy. Going for a walk reminded me of the time I jogged out the cow lane for exercise, to please Gloria Graham. I haven't seen her for awhile now. I sure hope she'll soon get over her mad toward me.

Walking in the dark also reminded me of the time I was going to the phone shanty in the dark and got sprayed by a skunk. Around here you never know when you'll meet one of those creatures. They're plentiful, and we kept our eyes open for them. So we walked hand in hand, Sadie and I, enjoying the closeness and the night sounds.

At Grandpa Dave's, we sat in their peaceful, homey, old-fashioned kitchen, eating apples and popcorn. Grandpa Dave sat in his rocker by the fire telling stories, and Grandma Annie sat knitting a scarf. They are getting old, and I tried to capture the scene for my storehouse of precious memories. ≷

We had a scare last night around midnight. I woke up suddenly, heart beating wildly, and sat bolt upright. What had disturbed me? Then I heard a scraping sound. Oh, the terror of hearing a strange sound in the night when just awakened out of a deep sleep! Then I heard stealthy footsteps on the stairs.

"Nate, Nate," I cried, shaking his arm and leaping out of bed. "There's someone in the house."

We both threw on some clothes, and Nate went to investigate with a flashlight. I struck a match and lit the kerosene lamp with trembling fingers. A few minutes later Nate came back and said, "The front door was standing wide open, but there's no one around now."

I went into the children's rooms, and they were all safe in bed, sleeping soundly. Then I knocked softly on Franie's bedroom door and woke her up out of a deep sleep. She had seen and heard nothing, and I wished I hadn't disturbed her.

Together Nate and I went through all the rooms with the lamp, looking behind doors and furniture and under beds. I had a feeling that any minute someone would come up behind me and grab me, or that someone was outside watching us. What a sinister feeling!

We saw and heard nothing more, but sleep was out of the question until morning. Franie said this morning that she also couldn't sleep anymore after I woke her. It's too bad that I didn't let her sleep. I could have spared her that fright. Now she's real jittery and declares that she's having a lock put on her door.

I, too, felt uneasy all day, and when I had to go to the attic for some quilt scraps, I begged Nate to go with me. He laughed at me, but he did go along up and checked out all the corners, behind trunks and chests and behind the old trundle bed. Tonight we securely locked all the doors, something we don't often do.

"Maybe the wind blew open the door," Nate suggested tonight as we were getting ready for bed.

Ha! I sure wish it would've been the wind. But does the wind have footsteps? Something mysterious is going on, I'm sure. Have the thieves from the trailer come back to the neighborhood?

The windmill clanged and whined in the wind, and I shivered in my bed. As we read our nightly chapter, the words "fear not" seemed to leap up at me. If "fear not" is a command of God, then it's wrong to fear instead of trusting that God is in control of everything. If God is in control, then we need not fear. What a comforting thought! ≋

December 14

Today we had church at Emanuel Yoder's. If anyone came away without spiritual refreshment, it was their own fault. We had a visiting minister, a kindly, elderly man. As he stood in the doorway, the sun shone through the window on his white hair, and it almost seemed as if there was a halo around his head. He told some Old Testament stories in a way that even the children sat up and listened, spellbound.

Then the preacher talked about church people participating together in worship. With tears in his eyes, he said that there's a couple in their community who've stopped coming to church. They say they can worship God better by themselves, and that all churches are full of imperfect and inconsistent people.

This is sad, he said, because all true Christians are part of one body. When we worship together, we link our prayers with those of the faithful. If we fail to worship together in a holy fellowship and become spiritually one with other Christians, we weaken the body of Christ. That's really *be-denklich* (thought-provoking).

After this Sunday, church services will be more meaningful to me. It's easy just to take this privilege and blessing for granted and fail to realize how sacred and hallowed it is to worship together in fellowship with others of like precious faith. ≋

December 17

*C*hristmastime is drawing near! I've already made twelve kinds of cookies and four kinds of dipped-chocolate candy. If only these goodies wouldn't be so hard to resist! I have a sweet tooth, and if I give in to the urge to nibble, the pounds creep on.

Next I'll have to go for Gloria's Miracle Diet Powder after all. But no! After the holidays I'll exert my willpower again. I've got to show her that I don't need her stuff, after that mug she sent me.

Yesterday the UPS man brought a big package. The children happily crowded around, each wanting to catch the first glimpse of its contents. There were layers of newspapers to peel off, and finally it was down to a small parcel. Little Crist begged to be the one to finish unwrapping it.

Shiny-eyed, he tore off the last piece. It was a white mug with printing on it: To Miriam, the _____ _____. I quickly covered the vulgar words with my hand.

There was a small card enclosed, saying it was from Gloria Graham. The whole event sure took the joy out of my day. However, I pretended that nothing was wrong, got a can of spray paint, and covered the bad words—but not my name, which I had protected with masking tape.

However, I couldn't fool Dora. She stamped her foot and growled, "That Gloria! She'll never forgive you!"

Later I pulled off the tape, tied a red ribbon around the mug, filled it with evergreens, and set it on the clock shelf. If life gives you lemons, make lemonade! Tonight Nate said, "Why don't you return good for evil? Send her something real nice and heap coals of fire on her head."

That's a good idea! I've been racking my brain, trying to decide what I could send her—something too nice for her to resist, something she wouldn't return with "Refused" stamped on it. Tonight I thought of just the thing. My rose of Sharon quilt! She admired it so much one time when I had my quilts on the line to air. It's never been used except for on the spare room bed.

Once Gloria told me she's been wanting a quilt for a long time but wasn't able to afford one. If that isn't a good enough peace offering, I don't know what is. That's just what I'll do. Something like that might swing her around.

I can't understand her, making such a mountain out of a molehill. I always knew she was touchy. But now that she has stayed away so long and ridiculed me with the words on the mug, I'm beginning to feel there's something more involved than just her grudge about the diet powder. I wish I knew what it is. ⤳

*T*he first Noel, the angel did say
Was to certain poor shepherds in fields as they lay;
In fields where they lay keeping their sheep,
On a cold winter's night that was so deep.
Noel, Noel, Noel, Noel,
Born is the king of Israel.

—*Traditional English Carol*

For several weeks the children have been singing Christmas carols and practicing their parts for the school program. Today was the big day for us to go and see them perform.

Teacher Franie did a good job (especially since it was her first try) getting everything organized and managing the program. The pupils sang with gusto and recited clearly, and no one forgot their parts. Priscilla was there with Miriam Joy and baby Bathsheba. (Will I ever get used to that name?)

Dora was in a little skit, one of a group of carolers that went to sing for an old man with a bah-humbug attitude about Christmas. His heart was softened by their kindness and gifts. Peter carried a lighted candle and recited a poem, "The Light of Christmas."

Sadie's part really took the cake. She got up front, looking so small and frightened, and timidly said,

> When I step up on the platform,
> My heart goes pit-a-pat. . . .

Then she faltered, either being too frightened to say more or forgetting her lines. Her mouth quavered, and two tears rolled down her cheeks, but then she finally said the rest:

> Everybody will look and say,
> Whose little girl is that?

Then she scampered away amidst laughter and applause. A few people asked me if that was staged or for real. It was real. I know Sadie well enough to know that. Afterward, they had a gift exchange and a baseball piñata.

So now the program's over, and maybe Franie will be able to relax more. She seemed tense and preoccupied this last while and spent most of her time in her room. We sure can't seem to get close to her. Doesn't she like it here? Just what is the reason? Maybe teaching is just too much of a strain for her. It is a big responsibility, having eight grades to teach. Maybe I should offer to help her with grading or whatever, in the evening. ⋙

December 31

Fast away the old year passes.
Hail the new, ye lads and lasses.
Sing we joyous all together,
Heedless of the wind and weather.

—Traditional English Song

Brrr! What cold, icy, windy, snowy weather we're having! The wind's howling around the corners of the house, flinging bits of snow against the windows, but we're all inside, snug and warm and cozy. On the stove, the teakettle's humming over the roaring fire.

Nate's playing tunes on his old harmonica, Dora's cutting out paper dolls, Peter and Crist are rearranging their farm set, and Sadie sits rocking on the child's rocker, humming along with Nate. Another precious scene for my memory chest. Happiness is having a family to love!

I have often wondered if our dear little Amanda can see us here, or is she busy playing with the other children, or walking with Jesus in that beautiful land? How precious is our hope of someday being with her again.

Last evening when I had tucked all the children into bed after their evening prayers, Peter called me back into his room. "Does God really answer our prayers, Mamm?" he asked anxiously.

I assured him that God does indeed hear all the prayers of his children.

"But why doesn't he answer my prayer, then?" Peter looked forlorn, and a tear dropped onto his pillow. "I've been praying for something for a long time, and I think it's no use to pray anymore."

I sat on the bed beside him. "What is it that you've been praying for?"

Peter, however, refused to tell. He looked sheepish and ashamed.

I told him that if we pray for something that would not be best for us, God will not grant our wish but instead will give us something that is much better for us. So we must not lose faith in God or stop saying our prayers. If what we pray for is not God's will at this time, God still hears every word we say.

Peter seemed glad to hear this. But try as I might, I couldn't get it out of him what he was praying for.

"You can go now, Mamm," he said. "I want to sleep."

Thus I was dismissed, and I guess it's between him and God now. But it sure tugs at my heartstrings.

In a few hours, a New Year will be ushered in. What will it hold for us all? That we do not know, but it's a comforting thought that God will not give us anything that's not good for us if we yield our lives and wills to him.

It's time to hie up to our cold bedrooms where we can see our frosty breath in the air and thankfully snuggle under mountains of comforters and quilts. I love sleeping in a cold room—all except the getting in and out of bed, but that luckily takes only a few minutes.

Sweet dreams! ❧

Reconciled

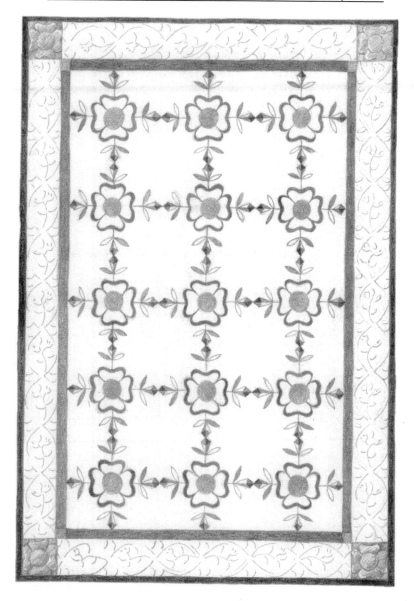

≥ ≥ ≥ ≥ ≥ ≥ ≥ ≥ ≥ ≥ ≥

January 3

Our dreams were not very sweet last night. We had burglars or trespassers again. It still makes me shiver to think about it.

I was awakened by thumping noises in the kitchen, and then creaking sounds. Nate jumped out of bed, grabbed a bathrobe and a flashlight, and hurried downstairs. But whoever it was must've heard him coming and escaped. Again the front door stood wide open.

Nothing seemed to be missing as we looked around. So once more the burglar was foiled in his attempt. But as the saying goes, *Es zwett dritt sich* (what happens the second time will happen the third). I think he'll try it again.

We'll have to be more careful to lock the doors at night. I think it can't be that we forgot to do that. I was sure I had pushed the deadlock button in the knob before I went to bed, but I guess I must've been intending to do so, and something else caught my attention before I got it done. Tonight I'll make sure the door is locked, and I'll pull the settee in front of the door, too.

All this makes me nervous and uneasy. What if someone is hiding in the house or barn this very minute? We haven't told the children about the burglar, but Franie knows. She hitched our horse to the trottin' buggy tonight and drove to the hardware store to buy a lock for her bedroom door. I can't say I blame her, but I don't think it's necessary, as long as all the doors to the outside are securely locked.

Franie even asked me if I think it might be a ghost. Her imagination is nearly running away with her, too. Next she won't want to board with us anymore. Yesterday she said she's lost fifteen pounds since she's here. It sure doesn't sound good for my cooking.

I wish I were the one who had lost that weight. I'd like to show Gloria that my way is better. I made a New Year's resolution to do without baked goods and desserts, and so far I've kept it. But it sure isn't easy. ≋

January 6

So far so good. We haven't seen or heard the burglar during the last three nights, and we're starting to breathe a little easier. But maybe he's waiting for us to do just that—let our guard down.

Perhaps I should say "she," for I'm beginning to wonder if it might be Gloria. She's the only one mad at us, as far as I know. I sent her my rose of Sharon quilt at Christmastime, and she didn't sent it back. But neither did she acknowledge the gift nor thank me. I'm really hoping that the mystery will soon be solved.

I've taken time to study a bit more of the *Wonderful Wife* principles. It says the man's role is to be guide, protector, and provider. The wife is to accept her husband at face value, look to his better side, and honor him as the chief leader in the home. The author says a man is more reasonable if he has the final word and is respected. Instead of always saying no, the husband then may want to be fair and generous.

That reminds me of something Priscilla once told me. During the time she and Henry were on the outs with each other, she sometimes fought to have her own way. She thought that was the only way she could get what she wanted, since it had become a habit with Henry to say no.

One evening on their way home from a work frolic, Priscilla wanted to stop at the grocery store. But Henry said no; he wanted to get home. That was unreasonable, for they really did need groceries. They had just learned that company was coming the next day. All the rest of the way home, Priscilla felt bitter, pouty, and resentful, and she let Henry know it.

After awhile she thought, *Is this the way a Christian should act?* Her conscience bothered her, and she began to make an effort to be cheerful and friendly. She even gave Henry a compliment. To her amazement, after supper Henry told her to get ready. Then he hitched up the horse again, and they went for the groceries. He bought her a lovely potted plant, and they had a happier evening than they'd had for a long time.

So I guess it's true that in a happy marriage, each partner must be willing to forgive, to try to please each other, to go the second mile for peaceful, harmonious living.

This morning I came across a poem in an old reader I found in the attic. It spoke to me, and I'm going to keep it handy so I can read it often. It's a story of a marriage that ended in tragedy, and there's a lesson in it for us all.

Almost a century ago, Will Carleton wrote "The First Settler's Story." The pioneer told about trying to wrest a living from nature, struggling against blackbirds that pull up the corn, too much rain, fires, mosquitoes, fevers, wildcats, wolves, bears, and rattlesnakes. His wife kept their little log cabin neat and helped all she could to tame the wilderness.

One night the farmer came home late and didn't like the supper his wife had prepared. When he went out to milk the cows, he found that they had wandered away, and he threw poisoned words at his wife:

You ought to've kept the animals in view,
And drove 'em in; you'd nothing else to do.
The heft of all our work on me must fall;
You just lie around and let me do it all.

His wife just looked him over like someone she had never seen before, with "sudden anguish-lit surprise" in her eyes. The next morning he left without his usual kiss. At noon he opened his packed lunch to find choice food and fresh pansies. He promised himself, "Tonight I'll ask forgiveness of her."

When he came home early, a thunderstorm was brewing. He found a note from his wife on the table:

The cows have strayed away again I fear.
I watched them pretty close; don't scold me, dear.
And where they are, I think I nearly know;
I've heard the bell not very long ago.
I've hunted for them all the afternoon.
I'll try once more; I think I'll find them soon.
Dear, if a burden I have been to you,
And haven't helped you as I ought to do,
Let old-time memories my forgiveness plead.
I've tried to do my best, I have indeed.
Darling, piece out with love the strength I lack.

The settler rushed out into the storm and tried to get the dog to track his wife, but the rain had wiped out the trail. They "dragged the woods" all night and came home in the morning to hear the cowbell's tinkling sound: the cows were found. Inside the cabin he discovered his wife lying, "with all her young life crushed and wrenched away, . . . not far from where I killed her with my tongue."

I could just weep a bucket of tears for that young settler's pain. How often do we give a scathing rebuke, a harsh lecture, say things in an unkind way, or even just thoughtlessly hurt someone's feelings! May this be a lesson to me! I think I'll try to read the entire poem at least once a month. What a burden for the settler to have carried for fifty years—"I killed her with my tongue"—that is, if it's true.

⪧

January 8

I think we have fallen into a rut here at our house, but we're trying hard to do something about it. After I read that settler's poem, I began to notice that we're all raising our voices to each other sometimes.

For example, on Tuesday evening I heard Dora yelling, "Peter, will you please quit pestering me!"

Peter yelled back, just as loudly, "I'm not pestering you! I'm just asking questions!"

She shouted, "Well, then, quit it while I'm studying my times tables!"

"I won't," Peter growled stubbornly.

I intervened just as loudly: "Children, will you stop bickering! Can't you live peaceably?" My tone of voice was loud, but not very calm and authoritative.

Later, Nate reprimanded them in the same way, I noticed. We talked about it and decided it's time we create a different atmosphere in our home, with less stress, tension, and impatience. I've heard the maxim about a child, "Make me happy, and you make me good." I must remember to take the time to play and laugh with them more, perhaps using some lighthearted teasing, friendly chats, a measure of praise, laughter, and joy, with God's help.

Which is more important, having all the work done, or having happy, peaceful children? Parents don't have to put up with bad habits such as bickering and fighting, if we take immediate and consistent action with the children.

Nate came up with the suggestion that we must all talk and work out our problems in a friendly, normal, conversational tone, and never raise our voices unless the house is on fire! The punishment for each violation will be a fifteen-minute earlier bedtime. At our house, that really is a punishment! Now things sound much better around here.

I think I myself have gone through a time of leanness in my soul. I was so taken up with Gloria's silly diet and then her spat with me, that I wasn't very spiritual minded at all. Sometimes, sad to say, it's a real struggle for me to set my mind on things above. I wish I had never even written about Gloria's silly case here in my journal, and then my childish joke on Nate at Halloween. I'm ashamed of myself. But I guess I'll let it here as a reminder for when I have a tendency to be "foolish" again. ≋

*M*aybe I have the new kind of flu going around that Pamela was joking about. It's called Amish flu: First you get a little hoarse (horse), then you get a little buggy. Right now I don't feel like laughing at that pun.

I have a bad case of the sniffles. I'm sitting here with my feet wrapped in flannel, warming them in the bake oven of the range, with a bowl of apples at my side. Outside, big snowflakes are lazily floating downward, and little Crist is happily running and shouting and trying to catch them. Oh, to have the boundless energy of a little boy!

I've been reading some more in *Wonderful Wife*. At first, as I read all a wife should be, it gave me a deep longing to be a better Christian and a better wife. But the more I read, the more I felt inadequate, lacking in necessary qualities.

The author says the wife is to have high ideals. She is supposed to inspire her husband to noble qualities and righteous living and bring him peace and happiness. This model wife herself must have deep inner happiness and peace, and also radiate that to others. She has a generous heart and is always eager to help the poor.

The wife is kind and friendly, never stooping to selfishness and pettiness. More than being merely a good house-keeper, she is a "domestic goddess." (This makes her seem like an idol!) The wife gives her man sympathetic understanding, accepts him as he is, and looks to his better side. She inspires in him a feeling of deep respect.

Sweetness and goodness surround her. On dark days, she casts light like a benediction. Her presence warms the home, and her smile has power to lighten that heavy chain of gloom that humanity drags along. That reminds me of "The First Settler." One line said, "She lifted tons with her smile" (Carleton).

Besides all this, she is fresh and joyous as a lark. Her approach is like a cheerful warmth—gentle, girlish, and trusting. She has cute little ways that stir a man's heart. This ideal wife is bright-eyed and captivating, with enchanting and pleasant ways. She is happy and vivacious, graceful and variable. When she speaks, she displays a delightful voice and a tinkling little laugh.

Putting all this together, she is anything that no one ever saw, and everything that anybody ever wanted! Oh dear, I give up right now! This is all getting to be much beyond me. I guess I'll just have to try to do the best I can in improving my character, to be kind, and forget the rest.

Poor Nate! I'm sure he'd like to have a fascinating, enchanting wife like the one described. Here I am, plain, fat, and unexciting. I'm *dappich* and awkward. I think I'll go and eat a piece of pumpkin pie, to soothe my wounded spirit. I'll put a dollop of whipped cream on top to make myself feel better. A scoop (or two) of ice cream would go very well with it. Since Nate doesn't complain, maybe I'd better count my blessings and be happy. Life can't be a continual bed of roses anyway. ⇗

January 12

*T*eacher Franie gives me shivery creeps. What charge does she get out of telling horror stories? And especially in the evening just before it's time for bed?

Her tale was that in a midwestern state, a young Amish mother was shopping in a supermarket. She left her three preschoolers outside on the market wagon and took her baby along into the store.

Suddenly a lady rushed up to her and said, "Hurry out, quick! I just saw someone grab your children and put them in his car! He's kidnapping them! Here, give me your baby! Maybe you can catch him yet before he drives off with them."

The frantic mother thrust her baby into the lady''s arms and ran out as fast as she could. Her children were gone, and so was the kidnapper. She dashed back into the store to notify the manager and call the police.

After this was done, she searched for the lady who had her baby. But the woman and the baby had disappeared also. The hysterical mother and the clerks searched all through the store. But they had vanished, and the frantic Amish woman discovered that her four children had all been kidnapped!

Franie said that a cousin of hers told her this story, but that's all she knows. There were no other details. She doesn't know the people's names and isn't even sure in which state it happened. Maybe next week it will be in our paper *Die Botschaft*.

I told Franie, "That's the most horrible thing I ever heard of!"

Then she started right in with another horror story: "This happened many years ago, before there were telephones, of course. The people it happened to never had any other children. A young couple of plain people had planned to go on a trip out West. They were undecided about whether or not they would take along their ten-month-old baby boy or leave him with their nearest neighbors, who had offered to babysit.

"Finally, at the last minute, they decided to leave him with the neighbors. They instructed their neighbor's fifteen-year-old daughter to come and get him the next morning. To catch the train, the carriage picking them up had to leave with them a few minutes before the girl would be able to come. But they told her they would leave the door unlocked, and she could come in and get the baby.

"They put the baby in his high chair and left. A few minutes later, the girl came to the front door for the baby and found it locked. Not knowing that they had left the back door open for her, she went back home and told her parents that the baby had been taken along on the trip after all, for the door was locked.

"Weeks later, the parents returned and happily stopped in at the neighbors to pick up their little darling, only to find out the shocking news that the baby wasn't with them."

What a tragic homecoming! I can't bear to think of them finding their baby like that! Nate noticed my stricken look and beseeching, imploring gestures. He finally took the hint, put his foot down, and said to Franie, "No more such horrible stories in this house. Don't repeat them unless you're sure of the facts and know they're true and the people they happened to. Someone might have nightmares."

Franie went off to bed, not looking very happy. Thankfully, the children already were in bed. I'm half suspecting that Franie made up those stories herself. Oh dear! ≋

We had a terrible fright again last night, after midnight. Dora came dashing into our room, shouting, "Help, help! A ghost! *Mamm* and *Daed* (Dad), I just saw a ghost running through the hall!"

She herself looked almost as pale as a ghost, and she was trembling with fright. Finally she calmed down enough to tell us what happened, but her teeth were still chattering.

"I—I h—heard a n—noise, and I opened my door, and th—there it w—was," she stammered. "It was either a ghost or someone wearing a sheet. I ran back into my room, and the next time I looked, the ghost was gone."

We tried to calm her. Carrying the kerosene lamp, we went slowly out into the hall, looking in every corner. The lamp cast weird and grotesque shadows of us on the walls, and Dora clung to me fearfully.

I opened Franie's door, and she lifted her head, blinking sleep from her eyes. She said she neither saw nor heard a thing, had been unable to sleep until nearly midnight, and had just fallen into a deep sleep. So she gave us no clues. Nate went through the rest of the house. He found the front door wide open but not a trace of a ghost.

Eventually we persuaded Dora to go back to bed. I promised to "sleep" the rest of the night in the girls' room, and Nate slept in the boys' room. Thankfully, the younger children slept through it all.

I'm beginning to think maybe we should hire a detective to solve our mystery—some kind of a Sherlock Holmes. I'm getting more nervous about it each time something happens, and then having to think about Franie's awful stories yet!

Could it really be Gloria sneaking into our house dressed as a ghost to scare us out of our wits, and then running out the front door and leaving it wide open? I wouldn't be a bit surprised. Her husband, George, has completely disappeared from the neighborhood. Maybe she somehow did away with him. Oh, now my imagination *is* running wild!

Ever since last summer, Gloria hasn't been herself at all. Surely a person wouldn't get so mad just about some diet powder! Something else must've happened to her personality, and I'm scared. Whoever it is must somehow find an unlocked window to come in through—or can ghosts just glide through locked doors? If it weren't for the assurance of God's guardian angels, how could we bear all this? ⋙

January 15

Peter came home from school ahead of the others tonight, crying and sniffling, and ran up to his room.

Now what? I wearily followed him upstairs.

"Teacher Franie's mean!" he sobbed. "She slapped me hard on the cheek, and I didn't even do anything wrong." He buried his face in the covers.

"Are you sure you didn't do anything wrong?" I probed. I couldn't imagine mischievous Peter being punished without a single offense. Maybe there had been so many minor offenses that finally the teacher's patience snapped, like the straw that broke the camel's back.

"No, I didn't!" Peter declared. "And I hope Franie never comes to our house again!"

By this time Dora was home and coming upstairs, too. "Teacher Franie isn't fair!" she stormed. "She slapped Peter just because he couldn't find his pencil. I wish we'd still have Ruth for our teacher."

At this bit of sympathy, Peter began to sob again. I finally got him comforted and told the children that maybe Franie is overworked and overwrought. They should try to be obedient and nice to her, to make things easier for her.

I've noticed this past while that Franie does seem tense and withdrawn. Maybe teaching just isn't the job for her. She needs our prayers and support. If she is overworked, she needs a teacher's helper. I'll have to talk to Nate about it. ⇗

January 19

*P*amela Styer has decided she wants to learn how to quilt. She stopped in a few days ago with a telephone message and saw the Dresden plate quilt we have in the frame. She loved it and asked if she could come here for quilting lessons.

Now is a good time to quilt, for the snow is flying and the wind is howling outside. It's cozy and warm here by the fire. Since then, Pamela came every afternoon, and we got to know her a lot better. She's an interesting person!

At first she quilted jerkily, putting only one stitch at a time on the needle before drawing up the thread, but now she's really getting the hang of it. She talks as she quilts. There's never a dull moment when she's around! She's pert and witty, and never once did she talk down to me. I wish Gloria were more like her.

Pamela told me that she and her husband are now divorced. She's getting really lonely and wondered where she could meet some eligible men. I thought to myself, *How different the ways of the world are from our ways!*

"I'm thinking of putting an ad in the paper," she said, "to help me meet that special someone. Could you help me plan it?" She stopped quilting and laid a finger beside her pert nose, with a dreamy-eyed look on her face. "How about this: 'Hello, handsome! Just waiting for you to come into my life. Seeking romance and companionship. I enjoy camping, reading, writing, and going to movies.' "

I suggested, "How about adding, 'I'm good-natured, kind-hearted, helpful, fun to be with, or something of that sort.' "

Those things are true of Pamela. But she shook her head. "That sounds too much like I'm advertising myself." Instead, she suggested, "Sir Lancelot, where are you? If you're an honest, good-hearted gentleman with a sense of humor, you may be Mr. Right for me. I love living in the country, going for walks, dancing, dining by candlelight."

Then she tried another line: "If you're a charming, intelligent, adventurous professional man, looking for a lady to share happy, spontaneous, friendly moments with you, then you may be my knight in shining armor."

"Oh, there's something I must not forget to add," Pam declared. "He absolutely must be a nonsmoker. I simply couldn't stand being surrounded by stale cigarette smoke. And he should be a really superb dancer." She thought a bit more. "It would be nice if he would also be distinguished and chivalrous, and hmmmmm . . ."

Suddenly I was startled by a piercing shriek, and Pam leaped up onto her chair. "A mouse!" she hollered. "There he goes!" She shuddered and pointed to the flying figure of a frightened mouse retreating underneath the couch.

Nate came into the kitchen just in time to see this little drama. With a big swoop, he lifted the couch front and stomped on the mouse with his barn boots.

Seeing this, Pamela shrieked some more. Little Crist, who had been taking a nap on the couch, woke up in a fright and began to yell at the top of his lungs. It seemed like a thousand chickens squawking and fluttering in panic. Pam, still shrieking, hopped down from her chair, grabbed her coat, and beat a hasty retreat.

In just a few minutes, order was restored and Nate was comforting Crist. But I sat there helpless with hysterical laughter.

Nate shook his head in a bewildered way: "Women! Will I ever learn to understand them? Especially *englisch* women! Imagine being so terrified of a helpless little mouse! Ei-yi-yi! She's almost as bad as Gloria Graham!"

Out the door Nate went, muttering. "*Deel Leit, deel Leit, sie sin net gescheit* (some people, some people are not bright)."

I blame myself, though, and feel terribly guilty that I didn't do something about the mouse sooner. For several days now, I've been hearing him in the walls and seeing signs. These past few evenings while Nate was still out working and everyone else was in bed, the mouse came out from under the gas refrigerator, twitching his nose, and looking for crumbs.

I usually set traps at the first sign of the critters, and it spites me that I didn't this time. I don't want to lose another friend. I guess it serves me right for putting things off like that. Something tells me, though, that Pam is not as easily offended as Gloria. I feel sure that she'll still be a good friend. But I wonder if she'll be brave enough to come back for quilting practice. She was so interesting.

In the evening after we were in bed, I told Nate about Pamela's advertisements for a man. He let out a few chuckles and joked that after he is gone, I can put an ad in the paper like that, describing myself as a "buxom, plump, Amish woman, with plenty of *Schpeck* (fat) to squeeze, and chubby cheeks to pinch."

He nearly got kicked out of bed for that, though. He knows I'm sensitive about my *Schpeck* and trying to live without shoofly pie, *Schnitz un Gnepp* (apple slices and dumplings), and other goodies.

I wonder what Gloria would do if I'd call her and tell her I really want to try her diet powder and her fad diet now after all. But, seriously, Nate really does not mind my fat. He just likes to tease. He says, "A plump wife and a big barn, never did any man harm." So why do I let it bother me? ≥

January 20

*T*his time it was Franie who was out of sorts when she came home from school.

"Those big boys sure are a problem," she complained. "They're so disrespectful. It seems like they're always trying to think of ways to annoy me. Whenever I have my back turned, I know they're laughing at me and making faces, but I can never catch them at it. I wish I knew what to do about it."

She slumped dejectedly on the settee and looked so utterly miserable and forlorn that my heart went out to her in sympathy. Franie seemed so discouraged, and I sure wished I could help her.

I asked, "In what other ways are they disrespectful and troublesome? Maybe the school board members could help somehow?"

"Oh no, no," Franie replied hastily and anxiously. "Please don't say anything to Nate! It's not that bad. It's really nothing I can put my finger on. Mostly it's just their attitudes. I'll take care of it myself. Please promise me you won't tell Nate."

Her eyes implored me desperately, and out of pity for her, I told her I wouldn't. She quickly went upstairs to change her clothes, and I was left to ponder what she said and to feel burdened by it. What advice could I give her? Why was she so opposed to telling the school board about her problem? Was it because she doesn't want to appear like a failure?

I racked my brain for solutions to her problem. As I did other things, I prayed for wisdom to say the right thing to Franie. I absentmindedly settled Peter and Crist's quarrel, helped Dora with her pie making, and showed Sadie how to make cinnamon crumpets with the leftover dough.

Later in the evening when Franie came downstairs, I suggested she could send notes to the parents of the boys, tell them about the disrespectful actions and attitudes, and ask for their help.

However, Franie looked horrified: "Nay! Nay! Please forget that I said anything about it. I was just tired. It's nothing, really." After a pause, she said sharply, "Forget it, I said! I don't want to hear another word about it."

She turned and went into the washhouse. I couldn't help but feel deeply concerned. The hard part was that I couldn't even talk to Nate about it. When I confide in him, he usually says something that makes me feel better or offers a helpful solution.

Finally, as I was washing the supper dishes and watching the moonlight glittering on the icy snow outside, I had a bright idea. I had agreed not to say anything to Nate, but I could talk to someone else—last year's teacher! I decided to write a letter to Ruth, explain the situation, and ask her if she would write to Franie and give her a bit of help and advice. She has plenty of experience and will be able to help if anyone can.

I felt a lot better, then, and the children and I happily went sledding on the barn hill in the moonlight. The snow was hard and slick, covered with a crust from yesterday's rain. After we spent an exhilarating half hour sledding in the frosty air, we came in with glowing cheeks, feeling invigorated from the fresh air and exercise.

Dora made popcorn and hot chocolate, and Nate came in, finished with the chores. We sat around the table to have our snack.

I thought of Franie alone upstairs in her room, and I felt sorry for her. It would be good for her to join us sometimes and feel like she's a part of us, in our family togetherness, but she's just not very sociable. I've invited her many a time, but she always declines, and then I feel guilty for being relieved. Yet I truly wish she'd feel at home with us, and we with her. How can I be a friend to her, if she doesn't want to? ≽

*P*amela Styer came down with a Tupperware container of homemade cranberry-orange relish yesterday afternoon. She apologized for making such a scene over the mouse and said the gift is for a peace offering. Imagine! We were the ones that owed her a peace offering!

I met her at the door and invited her to come in, assuring her that no more mice had been seen or heard. But she declined for then and promised to come tomorrow. True to her word, she did come this afternoon and put quite a few stitches into the quilt. She had along a newspaper column called "The Matchmaker" and waved it in front of me.

"Here," she proposed, "glance over these ads and see if you can find one that's perfectly suited to me. I think I'll choose one out of here instead of putting in an ad of my own."

I looked over the paper, and—oh my!—so many men seeking women, and women seeking men! There were headings like these: Hello, Gorgeous! Hi, Beautiful! Smiles are free. I'm cute as a button. High Energy. Let's seek life's bounty.

Finally one caught my eye that seemed just right for Pam: "Country Gentleman, sincere, caring, honest. Loves to dance and dine by candlelight, and likes nature and the outdoors. Seeking a loyal, good-hearted woman with the same interests."

I pointed this out to Pam. Right away she declared that's just the one for her. She's going to call him this very evening. Afterward I felt not a little guilty, helping her like that.

Maybe I should have told her (although she knows) that we don't believe in divorcing and remarrying. Did she think I was being inconsistent?

I felt so perturbed about it that I confided in Nate. He suggested that the next time she comes, I could give her a tract on divorce and remarriage. I feel better now that I've decided to do that. How thankful I am for a good, kind Christian husband! 🐚

I think I've finally been able to figure out why I don't feel much like writing spiritual thoughts and feelings lately. It's because of Teacher Franie. I know it's not noble and gracious of me to mind her so, but I can't seem to help it. She is so—so righteous. She prays longer than the rest of us when we have silent grace before meals, apparently just to show how spiritual she is. Somehow she is—just holier, or else she has a "holier than thou" attitude.

Furthermore, she has a holier-than-thou, reproving way of saying things. At first I thought it was just me, but Nate is minding it now, too. Last week one day she asked him (sweetly) if he doesn't think he ought to help neighbor Eli more, with the shed he's building.

Nate was not a little provoked and didn't give her a reply. "Here I had just kindly offered to get her a teacher's helper," he grumbled to me later. "She flatly refused my offer, and now she's trying to boss me yet."

It would all be well and good for her to be so religious and pray longer if her personality and character would be more Christlike. Tonight at the supper table when Sadie passed a dish of peaches to Franie, somehow some peach juice accidentally spilled onto the tablecloth. Franie scolded her severely for not being more careful. Sadie's eyes filled with tears, and Franie said, "Now don't be a crybaby yet."

Tonight she asked me if I didn't think I'd feel better if I'd sweep the kitchen before I sat down to quilt. Then she went upstairs to her room, and I heaved a sigh of relief. I know I shouldn't judge, but it seems to me she's self-righteous to an annoying degree. I resented her bossing me like that. We have the duties shared out. It's Dora's job to sweep the kitchen in the evening, as soon as Crist has picked up his toys.

I know I shouldn't let it bother me, but . . . it's easier said than done. I try to have sympathy for her, for I can tell that she doesn't like teaching and it's hard on her nerves. At the last school board meeting, one of the board members urged her to not be afraid to say if it's too much for her or getting the best of her.

She resented that and quickly said, "Oh, are you trying to get rid of me?"

Several times I've tried to have a heart-to-heart talk with her but was quickly rebuffed. At any rate, she won't be teaching school next year, that's for sure. But she means to stick it out and finish this term.

I copied something from a magazine that I hope will help me to be patient with Franie and not to complain about her, not even in my journal. This is the last time I'm going to spout off about it! Here it is:

Such a Little Way Together

At the family supper table, Mary shared an exasperating experience on the way home from work that evening.

"A woman got on the bus at 55th and squeezed into a small space beside me. There she sat, half on top of me, her bundles poking me in the face. I had to keep dodging so one bundle wouldn't knock my hat off."

Mary's little brother piped up, "Why didn't you tell her to get up, that she was half on your seat?"

"It wasn't worthwhile," replied Mary. "We had such a little way to go together."

Here is a motto for us all: It wasn't worthwhile. We had such a little way to go together.

How relatively unimportant irritations of the day become when, at eventide, we view them in their true perspective. The unkindness, ingratitude, lack of understanding on the part of our fellows—how much easier it is to bear them silently when we remember that we have such a little way to go together!

How much more urgent that we show patience, forbearance, and sweet reasonableness to those making life's journey hand in hand with us—when we remind ourselves that we have such a little way to go together.

We have so little time to praise God, who has called us out of darkness into his marvelous light! So little time to love God, who first loved us. So little time to live the gospel!

What a different world, church, and family it would make, if each of us would always remember: We have such a little way to go together!

—Herman W. Gockel (adapted) ≽

A letter for Franie came in today's mail. Sure enough, Ruth's return address was in the upper left-hand corner. She must have put a return letter into the mail almost immediately. Good for her!

I was sure Franie would welcome any help and advice she could get from an experienced teacher, and that things would go better for her soon. It never entered my mind that I would soon be proved wrong.

I spent the day making doughnuts, with little Crist's help, using up the lard left over from the last butchering. The kitchen was filled with the wonderful aroma of frying and sugared doughnuts, and I was humming a happy tune when Franie came in the door, carrying her usual big stack of books.

She took one look at the return address on her letter, and immediately her face darkened.

"What could she want?" Franie muttered as she tore open the envelope. She read it quickly, then said disgustedly, "The nerve of her! She thinks she knows how so much better than I. And who was telling tales about me, I wonder?"

Franie's eyes blazed, and then I saw something in her eyes that looked like a flicker of fear. "People are gossiping about me!" she cried, and suddenly she turned and fled up the stairs, slamming the door behind her.

With a sinking heart, I realized that I had done the wrong thing again! Oh dear! I could cry. I meant it well, but my plan backfired, and I did more harm than good.

Will I ever really understand Franie? How can I help her? My intentions are good, but I'm always zigging when I should be zagging, and vice versa. One thing sure, Franie won't confide in me again right away! I admit my mistake, and I'll chalk it up to experience. She doesn't want my meddling in her affairs! ≶

*J*anuary brings the snow;
Makes the feet and fingers glow!

—*Unknown*

We've certainly had our share of snow this winter.

January is nearly over, but there's no letup in sight. I'm glad today was our alternate Sunday. We might have frozen our noses and "toeses" if we'd gone for a long drive.

Joking aside, it was a good day to stay home. Especially since I was waiting for a chance to read a book that Polly sent me last week, about Francis of Assisi, a man born in Italy in the year 1182. I was very impressed with his life story!

While still young, Francis gave all he had to the poor and traveled from place to place. He was telling others about God's love, preaching the gospel, and living a life of holiness, gentleness, humility, simplicity, and poverty.

Francis didn't think Christ's followers should own any possessions, property, or money. To him, money was a curse, to be shunned as the devil himself. He was an example to others to live simpler, purer lives.

All this was a reminder for me to not be so material minded, greedy, and selfish. We strive for nicer homes and farms, fixed up and handy, more money and possessions.

Francis and his followers went into a chapel to sleep at night, and for awhile into an old shed, where each only had a small space to lie down. They prayed and fasted. They begged or did only enough day labor for necessary food. The rest of the time they taught in the streets as Jesus did, telling all who would listen to love God above all else, and to repent of their sins.

Once a leper came walking up the road a short distance away. Francis was put to the test to live up to his convictions. The putrefying flesh, open sores, and dreadful odor of the leper were terribly repulsive. In the past, Francis would have stepped back as quickly as possible, as did the other people, but he managed to control himself. He approached the leper and embraced him.

Francis was elated by this victory over himself. It was the final step in his conversion to a holy life. He said, "The Lord himself urged me to go to the leper. Since then, everything was so changed for me. What at first had seemed painful and impossible became easy and pleasant." Shortly after this, he definitely forsook the world and with followers began a religious order.

In Francis' time there were many who believed that full enjoyment of life depended on having many possessions. Francis, inspired by the example of Jesus and the apostles, believed the contrary to be true. He couldn't bear to see anyone poorer than himself. Promptly he gave them what he could, willing himself to be the poorest of the poor.

Francis' love extended to all creation—birds, animals, and even the lowliest earthworm. He believed in preaching the gospel to every creature, as Jesus said. Once Francis advised a gardener to plant sweet-smelling flowers, not just vegetables. I approve, since I love flowers!

He lived a good and noble life, but I wonder if he would have felt differently about things if he'd have had a wife, and children to raise. The book says Francis was attracted to marriage and family. He handled this by whipping himself severely with a cord, telling himself that this is what he deserved. He wanted to follow Jesus' call to self-denial.

We can all take a lesson from his life. I shall write a letter to Polly and thank her for sending me the book. ≫

January 30

*F*ranie usually goes to school an hour earlier than the pupils to open the draft on the stove and have it nice and warm when the pupils arrive. Then she has an hour of peace and quiet to prepare the day's lessons.

Shortly after she left for school this morning, she came running back home, with tears streaming down her face. "Someone broke into the school last night," she cried. "The windows are broken, books and papers are strewn all over the floor, and the walls are painted with black spray paint. It's just terrible . . . it's—" She choked up and ran up the stairs to her room, sobbing the whole way.

Oh dear, what next? Right away Nate kicked along on his scooter, out the lane and over to the school. He came back looking discouraged.

"She didn't exaggerate," he said grimly. "There'll be no school today. The books are not only strewn around, they're torn and battered. Some of the desks are broken. There are broken beer bottles lying around and tire marks in the driveway. Some young hoodlums must be in the neighborhood again."

He went to the phone shanty to notify the police, and then to the neighbors. They soon had a frolic organized for parents and volunteers to gather at the school to clean up and repair the damage. The police did a thorough investigation first, then we women sorted and repaired books, scrubbed and cleaned, and repainted the walls. The men replaced windowpanes, helped to paint, and repaired desks.

It is so hard to figure out why anyone would take pleasure in deliberately destroying someone else's property. I doubt that they stole anything—they just damaged things. What did they gain by it?

Dora and Peter were jubilant that they had no school, but Sadie wished she could go. They are out sledding tonight, coasting down the barn hill, laughing and shouting joyously, and running back up to do it again. I envy their carefree happiness. I can't remember what it would be like to have not a care in the world.

Franie stayed in her room all day, not even coming down for meals. I'm afraid she's taking this as a personal insult or punishment. I went into her room awhile ago with a snack for her, and she seemed quite depressed.

"I wish they had burned the school down," she moaned. "Then I wouldn't have to go back."

"Franie!" I cried, feeling shocked. "Don't talk like that. You know you don't mean that. You'll feel better in the morning when you see how everything's cleaned up and repaired."

"But someone must be awful mad at me," she groaned in a choking voice. "Someone must really hate me."

I did my best to reassure her that the hoodlums didn't even know her, and that this wasn't the first time something like that had happened. But I don't believe it did a bit of good.

"Be sure to lock all the doors tonight," she said worriedly. "Whoever is after me might try to break in tonight. Those ghosts you heard in the house—I'm sure now that it was someone trying to scare me."

She shivered. "I'm glad I have this sturdy lock for my door, or I wouldn't be able to sleep a wink."

I tried to allay her fears, but she has me all nervous now, too. Were those prowlers that left the front door open really someone trying to scare Franie? I'm feeling rather jittery tonight, even though we have new locks on all the bedroom doors.

Today I found out at school that Franie's story about the four Amish children being kidnapped in a midwestern state was not true. How such a story ever came to be circulating around, I don't know. But it seemed that all the other women had heard it, too, and for a while thought it was true. What a relief though, to find out that it wasn't!

Apparently the story was even circulating in other states, and this week there was a notice in *Die Botschaft* that it was entirely a false rumor, and nothing of the sort happened. I hope the other story about a child being left in his high chair was also a fabricated one, even though it was supposed to have happened so long ago. I guess we'll never know for sure. ≋

A misty fog creeps over the land, reminding me of a line I once heard, "The fog comes on little cat feet" (Carl Sandburg). Everything is damp and dreary outside, and I was feeling about as dreary as the weather.

Then Pam came to the door, ready to quilt again, with no more mention of her fright over the mouse. She was her usual bright and happy self, and I soon felt cheered up.

She said she called her "dream man" of the Matchmaker ad and plans to have a date with him on Saturday evening. Pam didn't say a word about the tract I sent her, so I don't think she was offended. I'm so glad she's not like Gloria. At least I feel as if I've done my duty by her now, even though our beliefs are different.

Pam wasn't here long until Priscilla came to the door with baby Bathsheba in her arms and Miriam by her side. And then a carriage drove in. Barbianne was driving, and she had Grandma Annie along. They had this planned as a surprise for Franie.

Ever since her school was vandalized, she's been feeling low, staying mostly in her room. A substitute teacher took her place in the schoolroom today and yesterday. When I called Franie, she came downstairs, looking tired and hollow eyed. She cheered up somewhat though, when she saw the visitors and the gifts they had brought for her.

Franie enjoyed holding Bathsheba and playing with Miriam. What would we do without kind friends and neighbors? They are like a balm in Gilead, a help in time of need.

My feelings of animosity toward Franie are gone, and I

have sympathy for her. I now know that the way she acts when she's under stress is not her true nature. Underneath her "suit of armor" is a fine person, wanting to be understood and accepted, needing the sunshine of love and acceptance in order to blossom. I will try with all my heart to do better, to be a true friend to her. ⋙

What would we do without kind friends to encourage and cheer us on our way? I feel rich tonight, for I had two helpful, interesting letters in the mail today! One rare and special, from Isaac and Rosemary in Minnesota.

They've heard about our dilemma, and they also wrote about a few of their own. Rosabeth fell on the ice and sprained her ankle, just when they were getting ready to have church at their house. In the afternoon after church, a group of little boys were playing in the milkhouse and did some mischief. That evening when Isaac went to do the milking, some parts of the milking machine were missing.

He found one part in the cow gutter. But Isaac and Rosemary had to milk by hand, without the milker. Then the milk didn't cool properly because a switch was broken. Isaac was up late trying to fix it. Finally at 10:00 p.m., he went to the phone shanty to call for help. A sampling of the milk showed it was unfit to send with the milkman, so he called a guy with a tank truck to haul it to the cheese plant.

I imagine the parents of those little boys feel bad about that. They needed some adult supervision.

The other letter was from my friend Polly, and as usual, it

was just what we needed! It did cheer us up. She wrote in a jolly and sometimes downright hilarious way. Part of her letter was interspersed with Pennsylvania Dutch phrases, spelled in the German dialect as it sounds when we talk. We all got a good laugh out of it. She wrote:

Heit (today) is *Gruntsaudaag* (Groundhog Day). *Denkst du* (do you think) that the *Gruntsau* will see his shadow? Oh my, *ich hoff net* (I hope not). *Ich bin bereit fer Friehyaahr* (I'm ready for spring). Guess *moll* (once) what I was doing *demariye* (this morning)? Making *Fettkuche* (doughnuts). *Was?* (what?) *Du wit aa* some? (do you want some, too?) *Kumm un bsuchet uns* (come and visit us). *Daniel brauch do ebber fer schpiele mit* (Daniel here needs someone to play with). *Denkst net es is Zeit?* (don't you think it's time?)

Ach, ich bin so vergesslich! (oh, I'm so forgetful!) *Die Hammlin sin aus* (the calves are out). *Schpring, Mary, schpring!* (run, Mary, run!) *Ich hab vergesse* (I forgot) to close the gate.

Demariye hen mer en Amschel sehne (this morning we saw a robin). Maybe *Friehyaahr is glei do* (spring is soon here).

Well, ich glaub ich besser uff heere (well, I think I'd better stop) before you get a *Koppweh* (headache) from trying to read my *Hinkelgratz* (chicken scratch). You're *meechlich kittering wie alles* (probably giggling like everything). *Un so ich saag* (and so I say) good-bye.

> *Nix fer ungute* (I mean it well).
> *Aus Liebe* (with love)
> Polly

Good old Polly! I get *Heemweh* (homesick) for her sometimes. I think I'll invite them here for a meal soon. That is, if they're not afraid to come. Will things ever be straightened out around here, and the mystery solved? ➷

February 7

We drove to town today, and Franie went along since it was Saturday. We had some shopping to do, and Franie only wanted to get some things at the drugstore and get a prescription filled. So she said she would wait in the carriage until we were ready to leave.

When we drove into the shed to tie the horse, I noticed there were no other teams tied there—it was just us. When we had finished our shopping and came back to the carriage, Franie was sitting on the back seat, pale and trembling.

"Are you sick?" I asked, feeling alarmed by her appearance.

She clutched at her throat and whispered, "A—a—man . . . was here. He . . . he pointed a gun at me." Terror filled her eyes and expression.

"When? Where?" Nate quickly asked her. "Where did he go?"

"About five minutes ago." Franie was still trembling. "He . . . he . . . told me to hand over all my money. When I told him I don't have any, he grabbed my purse and searched it. Then he threw it back to me and ran around the corner of the shed."

"I'll have to report this right away," Nate declared. "Can you describe the man? Was he tall or short? What was he wearing?"

"I . . . I just can't remember. I just simply can't." Tears filled Franie's eyes.

"Well, okay, maybe it will come back to you after a while. I'll go to the pay phone and report it to the police."

While Nate was gone, I tried to console Franie, but I was terribly scared myself. What if the man was lurking somewhere behind the shed and would come back to see if I had money? I clutched little Crist tightly to keep myself from shivering.

It seemed like hours until Nate was back, and almost as soon as he was back, a police officer was there. Since we were right in town, he didn't have far to come. Another officer arrived a few minutes later. They asked Franie a lot of questions to identify the man, but she wasn't able to answer any of them. She just kept shaking her head and saying she couldn't remember.

Finally they let us go home. Are we really safe anywhere anymore? Prowlers in our home, hoodlums at school, and an attempted robbery in town!

Tonight I begged Nate to take Franie home, and he agreed to do so. But she refused, saying she's going back to school tomorrow and wants to finish her term. Somehow I feel that she is being targeted. Maybe if she would leave, we'd be out of it and she would be relieved.

If only she would go! There's something weird about all this.

O God, our burden bearer, help us to straighten out the tangled affairs of our lives. We feel so weak and helpless.
≫

February 9

I had been feeling good that at least the children seem to be unaffected by all this. We tell them as little as possible so they won't be frightened. But tonight Dora came to the supper table with bright red lips and cheeks, and her hair pulled forward and shaped into curls. She had a defiant expression on her face, almost as if she was daring us to correct her.

I gasped.

Nate stared at her for a full minute, then said, "You march yourself right over to the washbowl and wash that paint off your face."

Without flinching, Dora retorted, "It's not paint! Food coloring won't wash off."

In a no-nonsense tone of voice, Nate ordered, "Go! If you can't wash it off, I will. And comb your hair back properly."

Dora went. But all during supper, she had flaming cheeks and a pouting expression on her face. After supper while I was washing dishes and Dora was drying, she was still acting rebellious.

"Dora, please," I implored her. "We have enough trouble around here just now without you trying tricks like that."

It was the wrong thing to say. She tossed her dish towel on the drainer and ran upstairs to her room. With a sinking heart, I heard the door to her room slam shut. Another weary sigh, wondering why we ever thought—(on second thought, I won't even write it). *Ball wollt's besser geh* (soon it'll go better.) This, too, shall pass away, I know, and it won't help matters to allow discouragement to creep in.

Later, when I went upstairs with Crist, Dora called from her bed, "*Mamm,* I feel awful about the way I acted. I don't know why . . . I didn't mean to, but . . ." Her voice broke, and she brushed away a tear.

I sat at the foot of her bed and let her talk.

"I'm so scared," she whimpered. "I heard you and Dad talking about that man with a gun." She shivered underneath the covers. "What if he comes into our house?"

Poor child! I wish she hadn't heard about what happened in town. It's a big burden for such small shoulders. I did my best to reassure her, to trust instead of worry, and not to be afraid, but I feel that I'm a poor model.

Was Dora trying to hide her feelings under a cover of rebelliousness? I know she has a heart of gold. When those occasional bursts of rebelliousness emerge, some painful feelings are festering inside. We talked for a long time, and I think it did her a lot of good. But, oh, I must pray for more wisdom, to be able to guide her and the other children into the paths of uprightness, to avoid the pitfalls of sin! What a solemn responsibility it is to be a parent! ⋙

February 10

*T*he old windmill is whining and clanking tonight, and an icy rain is beating against the windowpanes. At least maybe now the cistern will be filled again.

The children are all snug in their beds, but Nate's still out putting bedding down for the stock. Priscilla spent the day here yesterday while Henry went to a horse sale in another county. It was an enjoyable day spent in making potato chips. We made four lard kettles full.

I still had plenty of time to hold baby Bathsheba. She's so adorable—with a dimple in each cheek. Henry calls them *fossettes* (French for dimples). All you have to do is tickle her chin, and she rewards you with a smile! It never fails. Such a happy, good baby she is.

Miriam and Crist played together real nicely all day, too. They covered the Boston rocker with a quilt, pretending it was a tent. Toys and dolls were the furnishings, and each had a *Bankli* (little bench) to sit on.

Priscilla and I loved to hear their conversations—they were simply priceless. They talked of having a farm with *Busslin, Entlin, Hammlin,* and even *Meislin* (kittens, ducklings, calves, baby mice).

Once they had a little spat about who would be boss in their "home," but it was over in a few minutes, and they were best of friends again. Priscilla and I exchanged many a smile over their antics and conversations.

And now for the bad news—another ghost story. Nate and I sat talking and eating freshly made potato chips until rather late in the evening. Those salty chips made me thirsty after I was in bed, and at 12:30 I went downstairs to the kitchen for a drink.

While I was getting the water, I heard footsteps in the sitting room. Whew! I went up those steps faster than I came down! My teeth were chattering, and my heart furiously pounding. I could hardly do more than gasp, trying to tell Nate about it. By the time Nate went to investigate, whoever had been there was gone, but the front door was wide open. Escaped again!

Sleep was out of the question for the rest of that night. Again we searched every room without finding a clue. Franie and the children were not awakened, and I'm so thankful. It would've just upset them and disrupted their sleep.

Franie has had enough things happen to her that unnerved her, without this yet. We decided it would be best not even to tell her about it. But, oh, what shall we do? We can't go on like this, not knowing who our prowler is.

We went to town today, and when we passed Gloria's residence, she was out sweeping the front walk. We waved to her, but she turned her back. I'm still thinking maybe she has something to do with these strange goings-on. But why would she want to hurt Franie?

I can't figure it out at all. Will we ever know? The suspense is awful, but I want to trust that everything will be all right. Sometimes that's easier said than done. 🐚

We had a dinner invitation to Barbianne and Rudy's place today, even though it isn't Sunday—just for nice, she said, because it's Rudy's birthday. It was nice to have a heart-to-heart talk with her once again, to see the farm, and also to think of something else besides prowlers and ghosts!

Barbianne talked about what it's like to have "empty arms" and how nice it would be to hear the patter of little feet and baby talk at their house, and the pain in her heart when she sees other new mothers come to church with their precious bundles.

"It's not that I begrudge them their happiness," she hastened to explain. "It's just that it reminds me of my own pain and loss."

She was referring to her stillborn son, and I think I know the feeling. I still feel it sometimes when I see other mothers with a glutaric aciduric child, thriving and appearing to be in good health. Sometimes I catch myself thinking, *If only I hadn't . . .* , but then I sternly remind myself that such thinking is useless and even harmful. I did the best I knew at the time, and I will accept the outcome, believing it's best this way.

On her kitchen bulletin board, Barbianne had a list

naming Amish youth groups of this county. Someone had sent the list to *Die Botschaft,* along with the number in each group of *rumschpringing* age (at least sixteen years old, running around with the youth). There are the Chickadees, Pioneers, Diamonds, Pequeas, Pinecones, Cardinals, Souvenirs, Shotguns, Kirkwoods, Rangers, Canaries, Crickets, Pilgrims, Bluebirds, Orioles, Chestnuts, and Antiques. I think I have them all.

Each group has its own singings and other gatherings. Already I'm wondering which group Dora will choose when she's of *rumschpringing* age. There are several in this area that are rather "fast." So I do want to encourage her to choose one of the others.

Where one's friends belong makes a difference. Not just for Dora, but for the other children, too. However, I have a deep concern for Dora. Sometimes she's so temperamental. I hope and pray for the best in her life and for the others.

Barbianne wondered how I could stand the mystery and suspense of the goings-on in our house, and at school, and what happened to Franie in the shed in town.

"I don't believe I'd survive," she confessed. "I'd be shaking with fright for a week if I'd hear someone in the house at night. I think I'd move out. How can you be so calm?"

She sure wouldn't say that if she knew how often I lie awake at night, listening with thumping heartbeats for stealthy footsteps in the dark. I think I'm getting old before my time. There are dark circles under my eyes. I need to remind myself that we need not fear men and what they can do to us. God is in control of everything. ≽

*T*onight when Franie came home from school, she asked if there was any mail for her. This time a letter came with her name on it. I hoped it wasn't anything that would upset her like Ruth's letter had.

I was mixing cookie dough, and the children were crowding around, wanting to help. In the middle of that, I heard a shriek from Franie. "Just listen to this! I can't believe it!" She covered her face and moaned.

"Franie, what is it?" I cried, feeling terribly alarmed. "Is it bad news? Was someone hurt?"

Franie shook her head. "Here, read it! It's awful!"

I took the letter with trembling hands and read:

Dear Franie,

Meet me on Friday night under the cherry tree at the end of the lane. If you don't, you'll be sorry. Don't say a word of this to the police or to anyone else, and you won't get hurt. If you tattle, BEWARE!

The threat made me shiver. Peter was immediately sent to the barn for Nate. Questions tumbled over each other in my mind. Did the writer mean that if we tell the police, Franie would get hurt? To whom could we go for advice? What should we do?

Dora and Sadie finished the cookies while Nate and I discussed what we should do. Franie remained huddled on the settee, still covering her face with her hands.

Nate decided to hitch up the horse and go to talk with Henry about it, and also with Preacher Emanuel, and show them the letter. We knew we needed help and advice, but that threat, "If you tattle, BEWARE," stared us in the face. What would the letter writer do?

It seemed like a long time till Nate came back. I gave the children their supper, but neither Franie nor I could eat a thing. I felt too distracted and bothered, and Franie declared that food would be sure to stick in her throat and choke her.

Finally Nate came back, and I ran out to help him unhitch. I sure felt a lot better when Nate said that both Henry and Emanuel think it sounds more like bluff than anything else, a scare tactic rather than real danger. It doesn't quite ring true enough to be real. They think the best thing to do is to ignore the letter and do nothing.

Oh, I hope they're right, but who would want to scare Franie, and why? Will we ever know? ⪜

February 13

*D*ora brought an upper-grade Pathway reading book home from school. In glancing through it, I came across a poem that I liked. The title is "The Unbarred Door," about a pioneer man named Amos, and his wife. When they heard that Native American Indians were coming, the wife wanted to bolt the door, but Amos thought it best to leave the door unbarred.

I'm afraid I would have been just like that wife was. Since the last time we had a prowler, I always double-check to make sure the door's locked before we go to bed. I thought it wasn't possible that we forgot it again that one time. I had been sure the door was locked. But I was proved wrong when the prowler again got in and then left the door wide open.

Since I've read this poem, I'm wondering, *Would it somehow also be better not to lock our doors?* But I'm not brave enough to leave them open and find out.

The poem, by an unknown author, tells how peace-loving Amos with unbarred door let wandering Native Americans have shelter in his cabin.

One night a neighbor warned him to bolt his door because of raids and to keep his powder dry.

Amos thoughtfully replied,

> The God I serve
> Commands me not to kill.
> And sooner would I yield my life
> Than disobey his will.
>
> One gun I have but used alone
> Against the wolf or bear.
> To point it at my fellowman,
> My hand would never dare. . . .

Besides, the Indians are my friends.
They would not do me ill.
Here they have found an open door,
And they shall find it still.

His wife said she couldn't sleep unless the door was fast,
so her husband barred the door to keep household peace.
However, he was restless in the night. His conscience
rebuked him for having little faith in God. So he slipped
out of bed and unbarred the cottage door.

That night a painted warrior band tested his door to see
if his heart was still right and if he was their friend. They
went in and saw Amos and his wife sleeping soundly, then
left to find other prey. Years later Amos learned "how near
was death that night."

How I long for the faith and peace that Amos had. Un-
afraid, he trusted in God and put no confidence in a
locked door, rather just the opposite! God honored his
faith and sent an angel guard to protect him. This illustra-
tion stirs my heart to rise to higher levels of trust and sweet
dependence on God. ⋙

February 14

*T*he Dresden plate quilt is fin-
ished, and now I have a grandma's fan quilt in the frame.
However, it's not progressing very fast, for I haven't felt
like doing much lately. My spirits lifted when, this afternoon, Pamela Styer came breezing in the door, her thim-
ble on her finger, all ready to help quilt.

"I had to do something to pass the time until tonight,"

she admitted. "I'm sitting on pins and needles, and having butterflies in my stomach."

"Oh, what's up?" I wondered.

"Tonight's the big night, for better or worse," she sang. "I'm having a date with the man who may be Mr. Right. It took all the courage I could muster to make that phone call, but it's done now. Whether it's for good or ill, we shall see. It all depends on whether or not Cupid strikes. It's Valentine's Day, and that's a good time for love to begin!"

She was all excited about it and could talk of nothing else for awhile. "The ad says he's sincere, caring, and honest," Pam chattered on, "and loves nature and the outdoors, and likes to dance and dine by candlelight. What more could I ask? He should suit me to a *T*."

I didn't say much, but I thought to myself, *Oh, Pamela, he's probably an eccentric old bore.* Besides, I don't know what to wish for her. Couldn't she somehow be reconciled to her former husband?

It seems to me that sometimes *englisch* people separate for no reason at all. Don't they know that love has to be tended and watered and cared for like a fragile plant, or it will wither and die? That commitment to a marriage partner has to be permanent? That one has to keep on loving the spouse, even when affection fails?

Depending on the circumstances, feelings can come and go. I want to keep on loving through bleak times, when emotional satisfaction is low and negative feelings cloud the skies. Then warm and loving feelings will return to support the love we have pledged to give each other as long as life shall last.

I feel so sorry for all the children wounded and robbed when their parents separate and divorce. It seems so senseless and wrong, and against Christ's teachings. It's not as hard to understand in those who aren't Christians, or who are abusive or unfaithful. But it doesn't seem right for it to become the accepted thing in Christian churches.

I wonder how many Amish couples would be divorced if we had not been taught that divorce and remarriage is wrong. But I sure don't want to claim to have an answer to the world's dilemmas. There is so much I don't know or understand. Each has one's own sinful nature to contend with, and if we remove the beam in our own eye, before we consider the mote in another's eye, we will not judge others. ≫

February 17

*T*he children have Bible verses to memorize each week in school, and this is Dora's verse this week, from the apostle Paul:

> Whatsoever things are true,
> whatsoever things are honest,
> whatsoever things are just,
> whatsoever things are pure,
> whatsoever things are lovely,
> whatsoever things are of good report;
> if there be any virtue,
> and if there be any praise,
> think on these things.

I love to think about the good things in life: A father who is a spiritual leader of the home, working hard to provide for his family, and kind-hearted and good-natured. A loving mother who looks well to the ways of her household, takes time to teach the children about God and tell them Bible stories. Happy, obedient, and well-disciplined children. A single girl who is a handmaid of the Lord, ready to do what he bids her to do. A young man who is strong to resist temptations of the perishable things the world has to offer. The ministers, kind friends, teachers, and Christians everywhere across the land.

I also ponder and appreciate things like country living, fresh air, pure water, good food, our work and hobbies, a caring community and church. There are so many not-so-nice things that we can do nothing about. It's better not to dwell on such matters if we want to remain emotionally healthy, not tied up in knots by things like Franie's letter and our prowler.

I just made the round of tucking the children into bed, hearing their prayers, telling bedtime stories, and giving good-night kisses. It's the sweetest time of the day, when the hustle and bustle and little problems of the day are over, and all are safe in their beds for a night of rest.

Peter finally confessed to me tonight what he has been praying for, all this time—to have Amanda back! Poor boy! I wish he'd have told me sooner.

When I explained to him that God needed Amanda in heaven, Peter responded, "But *Mamm,* you said Jesus raised up Lazarus after he was buried. Couldn't he raise up Amanda, too?"

I agreed that Jesus could, but it wasn't his will. Amanda wouldn't want to come back, because she is so happy in heaven where all is beautiful and no one is ever sick or unhappy. We would not wish her back to this world again.

Reluctantly, after shedding a few tears, he gave up the idea of having Amanda back again. Oh my, I had no idea he was harboring such thoughts! What other unknown struggles may be going on in their little minds? O God, help me to be a wise and perceptive mother. ✑

*W*ell, Friday came and went, and nothing unusual happened. Franie went to school as usual and stayed in the house all evening. Nate and Henry together went out to the cherry tree and waited.

As they had thought, no one came, no one was around. Henry went home, and Nate came back into the house, pulled a rocker up to the stove to warm his feet in the toasty warm oven, and declared, "I'm beginning to think it's all a big hoax. In fact, I wouldn't be surprised if Franie wrote that letter to herself."

"Nate!" I scolded, feeling shocked. "How can you say such a terrible thing? I'm surprised at you!"

"I wouldn't be one bit surprised to hear that Franie has been our prowler at night, too," he went on, ignoring my outburst. "Did you ever think of it that Franie never hears the prowler? She aways pretends to sleep through it."

"Shh!" I warned. "Franie might be coming downstairs this minute. How her feelings would be hurt to hear you talk like that! Don't ever say such an unkind thing again! I'm sure Franie wouldn't do things like that. Do you think she would've ransacked and damaged her own school, too? Shame on you! You know how hard she took it."

"Well no—no, I don't believe she would've done *that*,"

Nate admitted. "Maybe I shouldn't be saying such things. Just forget what I said."

Nate's backing down like that, at least outwardly, made me ashamed of the sharpness of my tone. I apologized to him, but I'm still of the same opinion. Whatever faults Franie may have, I'm sure she's not a wicked person. She wouldn't do things like that, and it would be wrong to blame her. Surely sooner or later the mystery will be solved. ⋙

February 23

*N*ate left his *Mutze* (frock coat) at Grandpa Dave's on Sunday evening. This afternoon we drove over to get it so we'd be ready for the next church Sunday.

I was excited to hear a red-winged blackbird down in the marsh. The air smelled of damp earth and growing things. Oh, the happiness of the first realization that spring is on the way!

The snow was melting everywhere, and water ran in rivulets down to the creek. Something stirred in my veins, and I felt like skipping and prancing, or like a bird let out of its cage. I said just that to Nate.

He smiled, pulled on the reins, and challenged me: "Whoa! That I'd like to see! Jump out, and skip and dance alongside the carriage, while I drive."

He was in the teasing mood that I love, and suddenly I remembered that it's been a long time since I've praised him for anything. I'd practically forgotten all about it. Hmmm. I'll have to watch my chance.

On the way home we spied a familiar figure walking—Pamela Styer—and I suggested to Nate we could offer her a ride. I thought that even though she was out for exercise, she might be glad for a carriage ride. And she was.

Happily she hopped onto the back seat. "This is thrilling!" she exclaimed. "Just like in Civil War days. How about driving all the way up to Priscilla's and back, if you have time?"

So that's what we did, and Pam seemed to enjoy the adventure. I couldn't resist asking, "How was your date on Valentine's Day? I've been so curious. Or maybe you'd rather not talk about it."

Pamela laughed merrily. "You'd never guess!" She kept chuckling. "He turned out to be Gloria's George. I think my eyes nearly popped out of my head when I saw him, and he was just as surprised. We had dinner together, and I asked him to consider going back to Gloria, for she's pining away for him.

"Wow! Was he ever surprised! He said he won't believe that unless he has proof. I assured him it was true, and that Gloria actually told me so. He looked dubious and said Gloria was the one who ran him off. So evidently there was a misunderstanding somewhere. I advised him to buy her some candy and flowers as a peace offering. Apparently he took my advice, for I saw them together later, and his car's been parked at Gloria's since that."

It made me very happy to hear that they were back together again. I'm ashamed that I once thought Gloria might have done away with George. Oh my, what a great breach a small misunderstanding can make! Now if Pamela could get her rightful husband back yet . . . , but I know it's unrealistic to expect that. ✑

Dora seems to be growing lovelier everyday, if such a thing is possible. Her heart-shaped face, rosebud lips, and shapely cheeks give her a pleasing appearance. But, as the saying goes, beauty's only skin deep. It's the inner beauty and loveliness of character that's most important, and her personality reflects just that.

After her episode with the "lipstick," she's been doing fairly well, although I do see a trace of willfulness in her attitude every now and then. Once she stamped her foot behind Nate's back, when her will was crossed.

How can I instill in her how important it is to graciously give up her self-will? How much easier life will be for her and for those around her when she does that. She's a great help to me in the house, capable, and learning easily. She has the makings of a rare jewel, but time will show the channels into which she will put her talents.

Peter is a real farmer boy. He loves to feed the cows and help with the milking, to feed the chickens and hunt the eggs. The other day he brought a box of *Bieblin* (chicks) into the house and put them behind the stove to keep them warm. He's always the first child up in the morning to help with the chores. Sometimes I think his only fault is a streak of stubbornness which surfaces every now and then. But we can reason with him, and he usually gives in without making a scene.

Sadie's front teeth are out right now, giving her a cute appearance. She's still sweet and shy, and sometimes I think she tries too hard to please others. She's so sensitive. It doesn't take much to make her eyes fill with tears. She loves playing with kittens (just as Amanda did), dressing them up as dolls and even giving them rides in the dolly coach.

This last while little Crist is strongly possessed of a streak of mischief. He's so active, he keeps going all day long. I'm perpetually amazed at his boundless energy since he never takes a nap. Nate says he'll be a real worker some day. I used to call him Little Elf Man, but soon he'll be bigger than that.

Last week Nate hitched up the horse to go to town and pick up a repair part. Crist begged to go along, but Nate told him it's too cold, as he was going in the open trottin' buggy. When Nate got to town and was tying the horse, out popped Crist from under the seat, laughing gleefully. But thinking back, I don't believe he's any more mischievous than Peter was at that age.

There's a beautiful sunset tonight, a gorgeous red glow that makes the sun seem like a scarlet orb going down in the west, etching trees and barn and silo in dark silhouettes. The air is sharply clear and cold, making the kitchen seem cozy and inviting. It reminds me of the verse "Peace and Plenty, Home and Hearth."

The truth is that I'm feeling better and happier since Nate said what he did about Franie's disturber-of-the-peace producing just pranks or hoaxes. I'm sure Franie didn't write the letter to herself or prowl around in the night to scare us. But now, thinking that someone's doing this just for a prank, I'm not nearly as uneasy about it anymore. Sooner or later, everything will come to light. ⟫

I'm having a bout with rheu-
matism these days, with aches and pains and creaking
joints. Grandma Annie was over this afternoon, and I
asked her for a remedy.

"Put a potato in your pocket," she advised, "and then
when the moon is full, throw it behind your back as far as
you can. I tried it a few years ago, and it worked."

I quickly turned my back, pretending to be doing something at the stove, so she wouldn't see me laughing, for I
just couldn't help it. My shoulders were shaking, and I
quickly escaped into the washhouse, and on out to the
woodshed, so she wouldn't hear peals of laughter. It struck
me so funny.

As soon as I could keep a straight face, I returned to the
kitchen and pretended nothing had happened. Grandma
Annie was showing Crist a book, and then she helped me
peel apples for pies. I guess I can't blame her for believing
such superstitions if that's what her mother taught her—
and it worked! But I'm sure her rheumatism would've left
her without the potato, too. I guess I'll have to dress warm-
er and maybe buy some liniment. I'll sure be glad to see
spring arriving! ≽

*T*his forenoon I had a big ket-
tle of cheese curds on the stove. I had just added the ren-
net and was stirring the mixture when there was a knock
on the door. Before I could move to answer it, the door

flew open, and there was Gloria Graham. She came over to me, threw her arms around me, and gave me a great big bear hug.

"Oh, Miriam, I'm so sorry I was mean," she cried contritely. "So very sorry."

She looked truly humble and penitent, and I forgave her on the spot.

"I have an awful temper," she confessed, "and I was so upset at the time that George had left me. I wasn't myself at all." She kept on apologizing and rubbing my back until I was downright embarrassed.

"Let's just forget all about it and be friends again," I suggested. "We'll let bygones be bygones and pretend it never happened. Maybe it was just as much my fault as yours."

Gloria thanked me over and over for being forgiving and understanding and said I was an awfully good egg.

I must admit that after she left, I cried a few tears. Until our estrangement was over, I hadn't realized it was so hard on me. Isn't that what tears of joy are? You're not crying about the happy part; you're crying for the months or years before you had what you have now.

Just last week I heard of an Amish woman who had her eleventh baby. It was her first girl, a girl after ten boys. The first thing she did was cry. I thought to myself—tears of happiness! But now I know she was crying for all the years and all the times that she was disappointed. She now realized what she was missing, and it made her cry. Such is life.

Gloria stayed for an hour and was as friendly as could be. She's really happy that George is back, and I'm so glad for her. I hope she'll keep her temper under control now so he doesn't leave again. She reminds me of a part of a nursery rhyme I once heard: "When she was good, she was very good, and when she was bad, she was horrid." I think she'll appreciate George a lot more now and treat him right. ⫷

I saw the first robin of the season this morning and even heard a snatch of its song. My soul almost felt as if it had wings!

Today is Peter and Amanda's birthday—that is, if children have birthdays in heaven. All the children but Dora have birthdays in early March, so we decided to have a little party for them on Sunday. We let each child choose who they wanted to invite—Dora too, even though her birthday isn't until April.

Dora chose Henry and Priscilla and daughters. Peter selected Grandpa Dave and Grandma Annie. Sadie chose Barbianne and Rudy. Little Crist couldn't think of anyone to choose, so he threw his arms around Dad and said *"Ich wehl dich* (I choose you)." That was another scene to store away in my book of memories, a precious moment between father and son.

They all came. After we had our birthday meal, including cake and candles, and the dishes were washed, we got out the songbooks. We sat around the table and sang the rest of the afternoon, ending with "Happy Birthday to You" for the children. My heart overflowed with thankfulness and gratitude. When I think of families in war-torn countries, or starving children in lands of famine, we surely are blessed indeed.

Grandpa Daves stayed for supper tonight, and Dave was in one of his storytelling moods for which he is famous. With a toothpick between his teeth, he leaned back comfortably in his chair and related a few true stories of his own experiences. When he was a little boy, his job was to feed the flock of about twenty-five chickens every day.

One morning when he came out to the chicken pen, there was not a chicken in sight—nothing but a few feathers. During the night every last one of them had been stolen.

In those days no one was on welfare like they are now, and when people didn't have enough to eat, they helped themselves, especially during the Great Depression days of the thirties. The farmers were not hit quite as hard; at least they could grow their own food. But they suffered, too, for no one had money to buy their products.

Once he took a wagonload of his dad's pigs to market, and no one bought them. There wasn't even one bidder. So there was nothing to do but take them back home. He did a bit of business in town first, and when he came back to the wagon, someone else had put his own worthless pigs on Dave's wagon, too. Who wants to keep on feeding pigs that aren't going to sell?

So Dave drove through the poorer section of town, calling out, "Free pigs, free pigs," and got rid of them that way. Nowadays, I don't believe town people would know how to butcher a pig, but maybe if they'd be poor and hungry enough, they'd figure it out.

Grandpa Dave also told us a tale from his school days. One morning his friend Joe was late in getting off to school. He heard the first bell ringing and knew he had to hustle to get there in five minutes. His older sister Esther was just slapping together a sandwich for him. He saw several eggs on the table and told his mother he was taking one because he always had a hard-boiled egg in his lunch. His mother was in the sitting room, helping little Eli with his boots. Joe heard her reply something but wasn't sure what she said. He stuffed the sandwich, the egg, and a cookie into his lunch pail and ran.

At noon as usual, Dave and two of his buddies climbed out the window of the schoolhouse and sat on the woodshed roof to eat their lunches. Joe always cracked his hard-boiled egg sharply on the top of his head. However, this day it turned out to be a raw egg. It ran down over his hair, face, and clothes. What a sight! He was truly stuck-up. Everyone laughed because he was such a show-off, and this time he had messed himself up. After school Joe found out that his mother tried to warn him that those eggs on the table were raw.

Another story came from when Grandpa Dave was *rumschpringing* (running around with the youth). As the young people were gathering for an evening singing, a fellow was visiting who thought he was a big jumper. Instead of climbing over a fence, he took a run to leap it and a little creek on the other side of it. All this was to show the boys how nimble he was and especially to impress the girls looking on. But his foot caught the top wire, and he fell headfirst into the water.

"All this goes to show," Dave added, "that 'pride goes before destruction, and a haughty spirit before a fall.' It's much better to live humbly."

After Dave and Annie left, Nate and I sat reminiscing about Amanda. The memories are still clear, but no longer so painful. I treasure each memory of her now. She enriched our lives and taught us so much. Without having experienced sorrow, our happiness would not seem as precious and valuable, and maybe we would take our blessings for granted.

In my clearest mind picture of Amanda, I see her sitting on the porch steps with an armful of kittens, talking and crooning to them, cuddling them close. What a good little mother she made. The precious hope of seeing her again someday buoys up our spirits and gladdens our hearts. How could we bear it without that hope? ⧢

March 10

*L*ast night at midnight Sadie woke up crying and saying her head was hurting. Her forehead felt hot and feverish, and I went downstairs to get some Tylenol from the medicine cabinet, and the thermometer to check her temperature.

At the top of the stairs, I met Franie coming up. She was wearing a long, flowing white nightgown, and my first impression of her was that she looked like a ghost. Was this the ghost Dora had seen?

"Aren't you feeling well either, Franie?" I asked her.

Franie swished past me, mumbling a few incomprehensible words. Her eyes were closed, and I knew without a doubt that she was sleepwalking. She went into her room and softly closed the door.

In amazement I went on downstairs and found the outside kitchen door wide open. So! All those times we'd been badly frightened, it was only Franie walking in her sleep! Franie was our prowler! That was why she never heard the prowler. Excitedly, I ran up the stairs to tell Nate.

"We should have thought about that," he said. "She's the most unpredictable person I know. What will she do next?"

This morning I confronted Franie about her midnight walk, and she just didn't believe me. "It can't be true," she said in amazement. "I never did anything like that at home. Do you think I even went outside?"

She looked so woebegone that I pitied her. I assured her that she probably didn't, as it was raining outside, and she would've gotten wet. I had to think of the story about Heidi. When she was so homesick for the Alm uncle and her beloved goats and the Swiss Alps. When she was pining away for these things, she became a sleepwalker.

Is Franie pining so much here that she became a sleepwalker? Poor girl! No wonder, the strain she's been under! This time I'm going to put my foot down and insist that she goes home for rest. Surely we can get someone else to finish her school term. Enough is enough!

This morning she went back to school, but I'm hoping by tomorrow we'll have someone to take her place. ⪜

March 11

*W*ell, Franie won again. She's not quitting yet, and she went back to school as usual this morning. Sadie's much better again, but I'm keeping her out of school another day, so she won't get a backset.

In today's mail, another letter came for Franie. It had no return address, same as that other one, and the handwriting was the same.

Another threatening letter? I wondered. It bothered me all afternoon. Nate was spending the day at a farm sale, so I had no one to confide in. I was tempted to chuck the letter into the stove, but I couldn't be sure who it was from, so that was out. Anyhow, I didn't want to commit a federal offense by destroying someone else's mail. So I tried to keep busy and keep my mind off the letter.

Little Crist and I caught two big roosters that were proudly strutting around the barnyard. I took the hatchet and chopped off their heads. After dunking them in boiling water, we plucked the feathers and then singed off the fine hairs.

Crist was right at my elbow asking questions while I dressed them, but I was almost too absentminded to answer him properly. I was so preoccupied that I forgot to cut off the oil glands above the tail. I had the birds already wrapped for the freezer when I thought of it.

Finally, though, we were ready to carry them to the freezer that Pam keeps in her basement for her Amish neighbors. I hoped Pam would be home, for I needed someone to talk to, but her car wasn't there.

Finally, at 3:00 p.m., Nate came driving in the lane, and I went out to help unhitch the horse, feeling glad to see him. Crist was overjoyed to find a little red scooter on the spring wagon, just his size, and he went to try it out right away.

"Franie got another letter," I informed Nate. "I sure hope you can be in the house when she opens it."

"Ach my, her letters aren't anything dangerous," Nate scoffed. "We already found that out."

"Even so," I insisted, "someone is after her, even if it is just to worry her. How long are her nerves going to stand it? That's what worries me. Please try to be in the house when she comes home."

But as soon as Nate had put away the horse, a feed salesman came in the lane and stayed for half an hour. Franie came home with the scholars, which she doesn't often do, and went right upstairs to change her clothes.

The children sat around the table, munching their after-school snack of raisins and dried *Schnitz* (apple slices). Dora seemed troubled about something. When I questioned her, she reported, "Teacher Franie cried today in school."

"Why? What happened?" I asked.

At that moment, Franie came downstairs, tying her apron, and asked, "Any mail for me today?"

I was tempted to wait until later to give the letter, but I couldn't think of a way to get out of it without lying, so I handed it to her. I didn't want to watch Franie opening the letter, so I turned my back, feeling the suspense. I just knew it was another threat.

The next moment I heard a sound like a half-strangled sob, and Peter shouted frantically, "*Mamm,* guck (look) at Franie!"

I quickly whirled around. Franie lay on the floor with her eyes closed, apparently fainted away in a swoon.

"*Schnell, Peter, schpring raus un hol Daed* (quick, Peter, run out and fetch Dad)," I hollered.

I grabbed a bowl, filled it with cold water, and sprinkled Franie's face, but she didn't stir. The corners of her mouth twitched slightly. Then I grasped her by the arms, dragged her to the porch door, and stuck her head out to get fresh air. I sprinkled more water on her face.

Nate came running to the door, and just then Franie sat

up. "Where's my letter?" she asked, wiping her face with her apron.

Dora brought it to her, and she handed it to Nate, who read it, then handed it to me.

I read, "WARNING TO FRANIE: There's a bomb hidden in your schoolhouse. Do not go back, ever! STAY AWAY!"

"I'm not going back, ever!" Franie cried, crumbling the letter in her fist. "It's not safe! Take me home! Take me home!" She covered her face with her hands.

"Get your things ready, and I'll take you home right now," Nate told her. "School will be closed until we get to the bottom of this."

Wordlessly Franie got up and went upstairs to pack her clothes.

I followed her to see if I could be of help.

"I'm a failure," Franie wailed. "I couldn't do it. I couldn't be a good teacher. Now this yet."

"Please don't be so hard on yourself," I protested. "You did the best you could."

I wanted to comfort her further but was afraid I'd say the wrong thing and upset her more. In a few minutes, she was ready, and I helped her carry her suitcases to the carriage. She got in as if in a daze.

Nate took the reins, and called over to me, "I'm calling for a school board meeting at our house tonight. I'll tell Emanuel Yoder to send word to the school dads and the neighbors. You can start the chores."

I nodded, feeling a bit forlorn, and watched as the carriage drove out the lane and disappeared around the bend in the road. A robin chirped loudly and flew up into the apple tree. The air smelled of spring, fresh and sweet. I wished I had time to go for a walk along the creek, where

God seemed so close in the beauties of spring. But the chores had to be done, supper prepared, and the house made presentable for the meeting.

So, with a sigh I headed for the house. I wonder if things will ever be straightened out again. Has such a thing ever before happened to anyone? Now we're waiting for the parents, and I hope and pray that they will be given the help and wisdom they need to know what to do. ⟩

March 15

I'm rejoicing tonight that the mystery has been solved, and yet my heart aches for Franie. I'll try to write down exactly what happened.

At the meeting at our house, while the men were discussing the situation, Nate mentioned that he suspected Franie may have written the letters to herself, for some unknown reason.

The other men reacted the same way I did, with vehement disagreement. That is, until Rudy spoke up. He said that on Tuesday evening, he was on his way to town on the scooter when he remembered that Barbianne had given him a letter to put in their mailbox at the end of the lane. He'd stuck it in his pocket and forgotten all about it.

Not wanting to wait until he got back, for fear he'd forget it again, he put the letter in the school mailbox. While he had the mailbox lid open, he'd seen a letter addressed to Franie, in care of Nate and me. He hadn't given that any thought till later. Rudy was puzzled but figured it was none of his business. Not until Nate said what he suspected, did he think about it again.

The school board made plans to talk to Franie the next day. When confronted, she tearfully admitted everything. She had written the letters to herself. She also confessed that she had made up the story about a man demanding money from her while she waited in the town carriage shed. Such a thing had never happened to her. She had only pretended to faint when she opened her letter.

As she admitted it all, she sobbed, "I wanted so much to succeed as a teacher. But I was a failure from the start. I wanted everything to be perfect."

I've been thinking about that since and have come to the conclusion that Franie expected too much of herself as a teacher. She wanted to do everything exactly right. When she couldn't measure up to that, she felt like a failure. In despair, she started to pretend and play games. But then she felt worse about herself, and all this led to a nervous breakdown. You might say she plucked her own feathers.

Possibly she had expected to be a better teacher than other Amish girls, for she had taken some correspondence courses, and an experienced Amish teacher had given her some teaching tips. She took a test and earned her GED (general equivalency diploma for high school). But it takes more than that to make a good teacher. One also has to love the children and learn how to manage a classroom.

We've already found a substitute teacher to finish out the rest of the term. School was back in session again today. The children are making scrapbook pages for Franie, and the parents are making a sunshine box for her. Now if only Franie will be able to forgive herself and put it all behind her, she'll soon be on the road to emotional health and well-being. I'm sure that many prayers are being sent heavenward on her behalf.

Finding her school ransacked and damaged was another blow to her spirit. I think she took it as a personal insult, and it contributed to her breakdown. Her sleepwalking was caused by the strain she was under. We are convinced that she did not do it deliberately. Actually, she didn't even know she was doing it.

Poor girl! I had no idea what all she was going through. I'm so ashamed of how I resented her and how annoyed I was sometimes. I think I'll write her a nice letter. It will help her to know that we parents have sympathy and understanding for her, and that she is freely forgiven. ≽

March 25

I gathered a bowl of dandelion greens for supper. Mmmm! I can hardly wait to taste fresh greens again!

Now it's plowing time. I love to see the rich, dark earth being turned over, seagulls sailing overhead, horses trampling steadily, and furrows straight and neat.

I decided to take Nate a drink and catch him while he rested the horses at the end of the field. The outdoors was beckoning me, the weather was warm and balmy, a song sparrow sang from the fencerow, and two turtledoves flew out of a tree, kittering as they flew.

Nate's eyes lit up when he saw me, and I thought, *This would be a good time to give him a compliment.* I said, "I wouldn't mind having a picture of you and the horses there. It's a pretty sight."

He replied, "Seeing you coming with a drink for me makes a right nice picture, too."

He gratefully drank the tea, and I thought up another one: "I'm ashamed of the way I scolded you for thinking Franie wrote those letters to herself. You were right, as usual. You're so levelheaded, and you've got keen judgment. I'm sorry I doubted it."

Nate looked pleased, and I felt good as I trudged homeward. Maybe now that Franie's gone, we can think about other things and get on with our lives.

I spied some wild or forgotten daffodils blooming in the grasses beside the road. As I turned aside to pick some from the bank, a rabbit darted into the bushes. Clumps of green showed in the yard grass, and a robin sweetly sang from the cherry tree. It was a hard winter, and I feel extra glad to see the earth awakening to the beauties of springtime.

No matter what the trouble is, we can always say, "This too shall pass." As the Psalmist says, weeping may endure for a night, but joy comes in the morning. ◈

March 30

I found a few poems for a horse in *Die Botschaft*. I don't know who composed them, but I thought they make a good statement:

> Oh, horse, you are a wondrous thing.
> No horns to honk, no bells to ring.
> No license to buy every year,
> With plates to stick on front and rear.
> No sparks to miss, no gears to strip.
> You start yourself, no clutch to shift.

Your frame is good for many a mile.
Your body never changes style.
Your wants are few and easily met,
And you've got something on the auto yet.

—Unknown

All well and good, if the horse starts when it's time, and doesn't balk, and stops and stands when it's time, at the crossings.

Here's another little rhyme:

A Horse's Prayer

Uphill wear me.
Downhill spare me.
On the level let me trot.
In the stable forget me not.

—Unknown

In the spring, warm weather comes and plowing starts. This is the time to be careful that workhorses toughen up gradually from their winter's rest and don't get overheated. Horses can get into the fields earlier than tractors, and it's a little like the tortoise and the hare. The horses plod slowly and steadily, like the tortoise, but oftentimes get the job done before the ground is fit for the speedy hare (tractor-drawn equipment).

Experts tell us that farming with horses is more efficient and economical, at least in this area where most farms are under a hundred acres. Out west where the farms are larger, it's probably different. ⧽

*T*oday I made fifteen *Schnitz-boi* (dried-apple pies), with little Crist's help. Rudy and Barbianne are having church at their house tomorrow, and I decided to make some of the pies here to help them out.

It takes me twice as long to do things with Crist, but I don't want to discourage his helpfulness. He wants a turn with the rolling pin, to be the one to add the sugar and cinnamon, to taste it for sweetness (the best part), and to crimp the edges.

I found a poem that described Crist to a *T*, and I'll copy it here:

A Boy

A boy is a grin,
A tooth out in front.
A tousle-haired, freckle-faced
Cute little runt.
A where and a what, and a why and a when.
So neat, oh so good,
Then he's ornery again!

A boy is a noise,
A whistle, a yell,
A jet-propelled whirlwind,
Blowing pell-mell,
Endearing, enchanting, lovable, sweet.
A boy is a stomach . . .
His first thought is eat!

—Mary Springfield (adapted)

And here I have one for Sadie, too:

A girl is an angel with slightly bent wings,
Her halo askew, she skips as she sings.
A girl is sweet laughter with innocent eyes.
She gets what she's after, so young, yet so wise!

Crisp ruffled dresses, above dirty knees,
Gazing at blue skies, from under the trees.
A wink and a dimple, now gay and now sad.
A girl is a weapon, her first target is Dad!

—*Mary Springfield*

The part about being an angel reminded me of Amanda.
Her wings are no longer slightly bent, and her halo is not
askew. She's perfect now.

Sadie is sweet and lovable, but she has her faults, as
does everybody. Someday all God's children will be sancti-
fied and perfected in that land that is fairer than day. No
one there will have to struggle with a warped personality, a
handicapped body, or damaged and frayed emotions.

That reminds me of Franie. Every day I'm praying for
healing for her. I'll try to write to her often and visit her
whenever I can. She needs friendship. I hope I can be a
messenger of God's love to her. I haven't been her model
friend, but I mean to do better, with God's help. She is one
of God's children. Far be it from me to judge and con-
demn Franie and to withhold love and acceptance.

Friendship is like the setting of the sun;
It sheds kindness on everyone.

—*Unknown* ≋

*Y*esterday was garden-planting time. The frolicking breeze blowing up from the creek and the meadow was scented by fresh earth and woods and flowers.

I'm glad we waited to plant until the ground was really fit. Last year I was too impatient and planted when it was just a shade too wet. Later on, the ground got hard and lumpy. It was a pleasure to put seeds of peas, carrots, radishes, onions, and red beets into finely sifted soil and cover them evenly.

Before we were finished, George and Gloria came, carrying a big package. "I've never felt right accepting this beautiful quilt from you," Gloria said quietly. "I love it, but right away I knew I didn't deserve it. So I brought it back."

I was touched by her humility and told her, "Please keep it. Take it as a token of my forgiveness and friendship. You've done a lot for us already. I'm so glad that our silly spat is over and we're friends again. I can't bear it when someone's mad at me."

"Well, if you insist." Gloria looked relieved and happy. "But I want you to know that I was never really mad at you. Actually, I was mad at myself and at George, and I took it out on you." She reached over and patted George's hand before she continued.

"I'm glad we've forgiven each other and everything's all right again." After a pause, she added, "Another thing I'd like to do, is take back that awful mug I sent you. I can't believe I did that. I'm so sorry."

I showed her what I'd done with the mug. She asked for a Magic Marker and wrote where I'd spray-painted out those other words: "To a Best Friend."

We parted in glad reconciliation. Today a delivery man brought a huge bouquet of lovely, fragrant flowers from a flower shop in town.

It was all nice and kind of her, and I accept her sincerity now. But what about the next time something happens that's not to her liking? I guess I'll be a little uneasy until we build up more experience of trusting each other. But things could be a lot worse.

I'll accept her the way she is and take the bad with the good. Her flowers scent the whole kitchen, and the fact that I'm on the good side of her again is a sweet-smelling savor to me. I'll enjoy her good will to the fullest, while I have it. It's hard telling how long it will last. ⧽

April 10

A police officer stopped in today to tell us that the hoodlums that vandalized our schoolhouse are caught! It was a gang of teenage boys, the same ones that smashed mailboxes and threw eggs into Nate's beard! They also beat a boy on a bicycle and took his money.

When the police questioned them, they admitted that they thought the plain people wouldn't call the police, and they wouldn't be apprehended. I'm so glad they're caught. Hopefully that will settle their love of mischief for awhile.

≫

May 15

*S*chool's out! What a term it was! I'm so glad the winter is over and gone, and the time of the singing of birds is here. The children claimed that they saw at least ten bumblebees, and so it's time to go *baarfiessich* (barefooted). Each spring they can hardly wait for permission to do that.

The meadow is a carpet of green. Seeing the cows grazing in the sun-warmed pasture gives me a feeling of peace and contentment. I took a walk this morning through the dew-wet, lush green grasses along the creek, where the ferns were ankle deep and the yellow buttercups lifted their heads to dappled sunshine dancing through the trees. The fragrance was tantalizing, almost heady.

Once again my soul felt transported as though it had wings, in the midst of the splendor of the beauties of God's handiwork and his awesome creations. No wonder Peter likes to roam the misty meadowlands along the creek with his fishing pole. Whenever he has the slightest chance, that's where he goes. I can tell that he's inherited the outdoorsman side of Nate. He already shows a keen interest in hunting, wildlife, and woodlands, too.

When I was cleaning the attic, among Nate's things I found a copy of a composition he had written in school. He told about how much he loved to go fishing, and that it was his favorite hobby.

When I showed it to Nate, he told me rather sheepishly how he was such an avid fisherman that several times he had played hooky from school to go fishing, and had gotten away with it!

Maybe it's good that Peter has a sister on either side of him, to tattle should he ever try something like that!

In my poetry book, I came across the poem, "Would I Could Be That Boy Again." I showed it to Nate and asked him if that's the way he feels about it, too.

He read the poem, and replied, "Maybe I felt that way at one time, but not since I have a wife and children."

I thought, *How dear it was of him to say it that way.* I'll treasure the poem as a window on Nate's boyhood days:

> I love to dream of carefree days
> Of summers long ago,
> When the old mill stream would beckon me
> It's secret haunts to know;
> When as a boy I used to go
> Down to that peaceful stream
> To sit by the hour on the mossy log
> And dream and dream and dream.
>
> Barefoot? Happy? Carefree? Yes!
> Whistlin' on my way;
> Crickets chirpin' in the grass
> Singin' all the day.

Dust a siftin' through my toes
As down the path I walked;
'Hoppers' wings a clickin' so—
Seemed as if they talked.

An old tin can with worms I'd fill—
A willow branch would do!
Some string from Mom's old garden box
And a safety pin or two
Was all I'd need in the carefree day
To make my life worthwhile.
Would I could be that boy again
For just a little while!

—*Unknown* ≽

May 19

*P*amela came this afternoon,
asking if she could buy some spinach for a salad she's
making. Of course, I gave her all she wanted and told her
to come back for more whenever she wants. She has carried quite a few messages for us and done other favors,
and we have lots to spare, anyhow.

She stayed to chat awhile, as she usually does. I gave her
a cup of freshly brewed meadow tea, and she said she'll
never drink Lipton tea again. Again she brought up the
subject of being a host family for a German girl or other
exchange student next year.

I talked to Nate about it tonight, and I'm inclined to
think that we'll give her an affirmative reply. After all, it

probably wouldn't be worse than having Franie here.

I'm so glad the relationship between Franie and me is better now. The ice between us seems to be broken, and I feel as if a treasured friendship is brewing between us. We're exchanging letters regularly now, and I've gone to see her several times. The strain is all off her now, and she's much more free and natural. I'm only beginning to know the real Franie, and I like what I see. I feel that we're building a rainbow-colored bridge of friendship between us that will last a lifetime, as it says in this poem:

Friendship Is Love

Friendship is love and mutual faith
Receiving, sharing too;
Never demanding, just understanding,
Comforting, tender and true.

Friendship is a gentle, fragile thing,
Yet tenuous and strong.
It reached out and reaches far
And lasts a whole life long.

And when the light of friendship shines
On rain, in clouds nearby,
Then lovely bands of color arch
A rainbow in life's sky.

—Unknown

We've had our share of clouds and ups and downs as our friendship was struggling to bud, but at last I feel as if it's bursting into full bloom. It gives me a happy feeling, for friendship is love and good will. When these abound, we can obey God's command to "Love your neighbor as yourself." ⧽

*D*ora came into the house today with scarlet roses twined into her hair and a wreath of them around her neck. The effect was so startling that for several moments I stood open-mouthed and stared. Who but Dora would think to try to doll up herself like that?

I felt a twinge of sadness, sensing that the "little girl Dora" is gone, and a young lady is taking her place. Am I wise enough, and capable of being a mother to her?

This summer she's working for Priscilla three days a week and loving every minute of it. Caring for baby Bathsheba is what she loves best; she never seems to tire of it. Sometimes I think, or rather feel sure of it, that Dora and Priscilla are closer to each other than Dora and I are, and I feel a twinge of jealousy. But since Priscilla is her birth mother, that's only natural and perhaps destined to be so. Priscilla freely gave Dora into our care before she married Henry.

I dearly love my adopted daughter Dora and will not begrudge her preference for Priscilla. It's a blessing from God that it is so, and a cherishable, precious gift for them both. Truly, God does all things well. I believe Dora will blossom into sweet and gracious womanhood that far surpasses my abilities and talents. I hope she will be a blessing to all those whom her life touches. God grant that it may be so.
⧽

Our horse has the strangles (bacterial infection), so we couldn't go on our planned trip to church at Allen and Polly's house, in a neighboring district. I was sorely disappointed, but I guess it was good for me to give up my will in the matter.

We had a lovely day at home, taking a long walk together as a family. It's sweet-smelling honeysuckle time. Road banks are covered with them, along with shy, sweet wild roses. We met Rudy and Barbianne, out for a stroll, too, and they joined us.

They told us that a teacher has been found for our school—a nineteen-year-old boy, Melvin Yoder. He needs a place to board, close to the school, and the directors are planning to ask us. We've already given our word to Pam for the German girl, so now what? Barbianne and Rudy think they could probably take in the teacher as a boarder. I hope they do, for that would solve our dilemma.

My, that will seem different, having a young man as our children's teacher. I wonder what he's like. Maybe he's the studious, bookish type, wearing horn-rimmed glasses. I can't imagine an athletic, outdoor type, or a farmer, sitting at a desk, teaching children for nine months. But I may be in for a surprise. We'll just have to wait and see. ➢

I just don't know what's come over Nate. He's different somehow, kinder, and more loving and helpful. I'm sitting here worrying about it tonight.

Several times I saw him wordlessly staring at me. Does Nate know something I don't know? Does he think I'm going to die soon or something like that? He helps with the dishes, he thanks me and compliments me on the meals I serve, and he brought me a lovely bouquet of June lilies from the garden. He brought in the laundry off the line and even helped to fold it.

He's extra kind, helpful, and tender with the children, too. Last night he asked us if we all want to go for a boat ride. We rowed upstream to where the willows formed an arch overhead, then floated gently downstream in the beauties of the mellow June twilight. Myriads of fireflies twinkled along the shore grasses. All was peaceful and quiet, with only an occasional splash of a jumping fish or the call of a night bird breaking the silence.

Little Crist fell asleep on my lap, and Sadie leaned sleepily against me. I should have felt glad and contented, but instead there was a feeling of foreboding or dread in my breast. What was that about?

Nate was silent and distant, as if his thoughts were far away. When we got to bed, he didn't sleep. He tossed and turned, and tossed and turned some more.

Finally I said, "Nate, please tell me what's troubling you. Did you find some more tax bills that aren't paid? Did you do something you shouldn't have done? Please tell me."

"No, no, nothing of the sort," Nate quickly protested. "I don't want to worry you. Go to sleep and forget about it. It's probably nothing anyway. I'm going to sleep now, and you do the same." He rolled over on his side to sleep, but I was not so easily deterred.

"Please, Nate, you've got to tell me," I begged. "I can't stand not knowing. Something's bothering you."

"Forget it, I said," Nate said forcefully. "Relax and go to sleep."

Having decided to put whatever was troubling him out of his mind and to go to sleep, that's just what he did. Soon his deep, even breathing told me he was deep in slumber, but sleep was out of the question for me. I can't just decide to put my troubles out of my mind and go right to sleep, like Nate does. I lay awake for a long time, wondering about him.

Then today he was just as extra kind and thoughtful as yesterday. He helped pick the late strawberries and even capped them for me. We had an early morning thundershower, and it rained on several acres of hay that Nate mowed yesterday. He didn't even seem perturbed by it like he usually would have been, fretting and stewing. He only said, "*So geht's wann gut geht* (that's the way it goes when it goes well)."

He offered to put up the shelf behind the range that I've been hinting to have for awhile already. He had Peter fetch the hammer and nails, and now the shelf is up, covered with new scallop-edged shelf paper. On it I put Gloria's mug, filled with water and a bouquet of wildflowers Crist brought for me, along with the children's painted plates they got from Teacher Ruth. It gives the kitchen a homey, cheerful effect.

Nate's still extra nice, but whatever it was that was bothering him, he seems to have put it out of his mind. He's real cheerful now, too. Maybe it was just that my giving him compliments has finally paid off and brought forth fruit. But for some reason or other, I liked him better the way he was. I declare, I sure must be plain hard to please!

*T*his morning Nate came in and asked if I could help him sort and load some pigs for market. The children had all gone to help Grandpa Dave *blicke Arebse* (shell peas) for canning, so there was no one left but me to chase the pigs. It's a job I don't particularly relish, but it has to be done, like it or not. The truck would soon be here. I pulled on my barn boots and soon was in the midst of the activity.

"Hiya! Hiya! Hup! Hup!" yelled Nate, swinging his club. The pigs seemed to want to go everywhere but where they were supposed to. They say pigs are among the most intelligent animals, but I maintain they are also the orneriest, contrariest, and stubbornest.

Finally they were all sorted, in the proper pens, and ready to be herded up the chute and into the truck. This part was easier, until only one boar was left. He was determined not to be chased into the truck. We yelled and ran and clubbed him, to no avail. I grabbed the barn broom, and when he came in my direction, I aimed to whack him one. Instead he dodged and I missed him, and he made a dash straight for my legs.

I wasn't quick enough to avoid him, fell on top of the hog, and then got a wild, undignified ride to the other side of the pen! My arms and legs were flailing, and I'm sure it did make a funny sight. However, Nate wouldn't have had to laugh like he did. He simply roared, bending forward, then backward. "Ho, ho, ho! Ha, ha, ha! He, he, he!"

Now I was mad, really mad. At that moment my brain coughed up information from *Wonderful Wife*. What had it said to do when you are not treated with dignity and respect? I didn't think twice, I just did it. But sad to say, the teapot didn't boil over gently, like the book said; it exploded. It wasn't just mostly pretense; it was real anger.

"Nate, you horrid man," I cried. "You big mean brute. I'm never going to talk to you again."

With hands on hips, I stamped my foot. "How can you treat me like this!"

I glared at him and stalked (not swished) out of the barn. I was covered with bits of manure and smelled awful. Feeling mean and miserable, to the house I went, to get out of those filthy clothes and take a bath. I surely was filthy, but I felt even more rotten on the inside than I was on the outside.

By the time the water was hot and the washtub filled, I was filled with remorse and disgusted with myself. Why had I ever even bought that book? Why did I lose my temper like that? My anger had all dissolved by then, and I thought, *Poor Nate! Why did I talk to him like that, just after he was trying to be extra nice and kind these last few days?* I wanted to flop on my bed and cry, but first I had to get clean.

Somehow Nate got the pigs loaded with the help of the truck driver. After the truck left, he came into the house. "Heat enough water for me to take a bath, too," he told me. "I've made a doctor appointment for myself at 10:30, and you're going along. I want the doctor to see you, too."

"What? Why? Whatever for?" I stammered in amazement. "There's nothing wrong with me."

"You've never scolded me like that before," Nate commented. "It doesn't seem like you at all. There must be something wrong. Aren't you feeling well, or do you really feel so badly toward me?"

I looked at Nate standing there, strawhat in hand, an anxious expression on his face, just like Peter when he's worried. Suddenly I felt a rush of sympathy for the hurt little boy within him. I knew it was high time for me to explain. I reached under the mattress, pulled out the *Wonderful Wife* book, and turned to the chapter on childlike sauciness.

"See here," I told him. "This is a book for women. It says how to be charming and fascinating. It tells us what to do when we're hurt or insulted, to show sauciness in a childlike way. I never expected to use that part, but when I saw you laughing like that, I lost my temper and spoke in real anger. I'm very sorry, I really am."

Nate took the book, walked over to the stove, lifted the lid, and dropped it in. "So that's what it was! No wonder, reading such trash. I'm surprised at you!"

"Oh no," I protested. "There's a whole lot of good in that book. It was even recommended in *Family Life* magazine. I just lost my temper and used something in the book as an excuse. It was my fault, not the book's. If it would've been childlike cuteness instead of real anger—"

"Childish is right!" Nate interrupted emphatically. "Ei, yi, yi! You're a grown-up, not a child!"

I soon realized it was no use to explain further. There was no fire in the stove anyway.

Then Nate tried to make things right. "I'm sorry I laughed at you. I couldn't help it. You looked so cute riding that boar." He began to laugh again. This time I laughed with him, though.

"But why did you make a doctor appointment for yourself?" I asked, puzzled. "Aren't you feeling well?"

Nate's expression sobered, and he took off his shirt.

"Come here and I'll show you," he said. "There's a lump under my arm. I just noticed it a few days ago, and it seems to be getting bigger. I wasn't going to worry you about it until I know whether or not it's serious. But now that I told you I'm going to the doctor, I decided to tell you why after all. Maybe it's just some kind of a cyst or fatty tumor, so don't worry about it yet."

Don't worry! How does one do that in such a case? I wonder. I felt awful. I just kept hearing myself saying those unkind words to Nate, over and over. Now I know, to a certain extent, how that first settler felt, the one in the poem who scolded his wife for not keeping track of the cows. Then he lost his wife and lived in anguish.

> Boys flying kites haul in their white-winged birds.
> You can't do that when you're flying words.
> Careful with fire is good advice we know,
> Careful with words is ten times doubly so.
> Thoughts unexpressed may sometimes fall back dead.
> But God himself can't kill them when they're said.

> *—Carleton*

Why did I say those awful things? Even though Nate forgives me a thousand times over, they still can't be unsaid. I felt somewhat better when Nate came home from the doctor and reported that the doctor plans to remove the lump right there in the office, under local anesthesia. That doesn't sound as if it would be too bad. He has an appointment for next Monday.

So we're sitting on pins and needles, as Pam once said, hoping for the best. Nate is taking it calmly, after those few days of fear just after he discovered the lump. He's his usual self again, and I am pretending to be my usual self, pushing those anxious thoughts to the back of my mind. *Surely everything will be all right,* I keep telling myself. Nate has always been a tower of strength. How could we do without him? Now I know for sure that I have to be a grown-up and not play at being a child-wife. ≋

June 30

*R*udy is here, milking the cows. Henry is baling hay, and Grandpa Dave is managing everything. Barbianne is here, too, and Priscilla and Grandma Annie. They're making raspberry jelly and cheering up all of us. What would we do without kind friends and neighbors?

Nate had the lump removed yesterday in the doctor's office, as planned. The doctor told me it would take about half an hour, and I waited and fidgeted and waited some more. An hour passed, then two hours, and my fear increased by the minute. I wished I had brought someone with me to talk to. What was happening? What were they doing to Nate?

Finally the nurse came and ushered me in. She wasn't smiling, and neither was the doctor. He was wiping his brow and looked rather weary. Nate lay quietly with his eyes closed. Fear swept over me, and I sank into a chair.

"There was a lot more to it than I thought," the doctor admitted. "If I had known the size of it, I would have put him into the hospital to have it removed. The growth I took out was the size of a golf ball, and it had long roots or feelers. It was hard work removing it all in one piece. We're sending it to the lab for biopsy."

I swallowed hard and asked in a small, frightened voice, "Do you think it's serious?"

"It could be." The doctor was frank. "But we can't tell until we have the test returns next week."

Next week! How can I bear the suspense that long? It will be a long week, I'm afraid. I had to drive the horse home alone, and I sent Pam to bring Nate home in the back seat of her station wagon. He was very sore and uncomfortable and went straight to bed. Today he's sitting up, but sorer than ever.

I haven't much hope that the growth wasn't cancerous. A cyst or a benign tumor wouldn't put out roots like that. The doctor didn't give me one word of hope that it's probably benign. I'm frightened, and I can't talk about it with Nate because I don't want to make him feel worse. How will I bear the rest of the week? O God, help us all! ≽

July 2

*T*here's an ache in my heart that won't go away these days. I keep thinking, *If only it's not cancer, I'll never take Nate for granted again.* I'll be the most loving, kindhearted wife any man ever had. I'll never complain about anything. I'll cherish and appreciate him. I'll always try to please him instead of pleasing myself. I'll never say a sharp or unkind word to him. I'll honor him and have sympathetic understanding for him.

How I regret the tongue-lashing I gave Nate there in the pigpen! I've been assured of his forgiveness, but the scene still haunts me. I want to have a chance to make it up to him.

Last night I dreamed I was a widow, alone and frightened. When I reached over to find Nate, he was not there. Is this an omen? He had gone to get himself a glass of water and an aspirin. But maybe it was a sign to prepare me for the worst. Don't dreams fairly often come true?

I can't eat; food doesn't taste good. I thought it would be great to be losing weight, but I'd choose health and plumpness any day. I'll never complain about my weight again!

Never before have I realized how heavy it would be to think of giving up Nate, to review how much he means to me. *If only it's not cancer!* But I have a foreboding that it's serious, life threatening, and I can't shake off that feeling. I am not above making promises—

> I'll leave no tender word unsaid.
> Do good while life shall last.
> I know the mill can never grind
> With the water that is past.

To ward off desperation, I searched for comfort in God's promises through the prophet Isaiah: "When you pass through the waters, I will be with you, and through the rivers, they shall not overflow you: when you walk through the fire, you shall not be burned; neither shall the flame kindle upon you." ⦚

Once more I've come to the end of my journal—the last page. What will the future hold? I must be brave and strong; I must trust. I'm trying to live up to Job's faith: "Though God slay me, yet will I trust in him."

I have many cherished memories, much to be thankful for. I have my precious family, loaned to me for a little while. In fact, everything I have belongs to the Lord. He has given it, and if he chooses to take it again, I will say with Job, "The Lord gave, and the Lord has taken away; blessed be the name of the Lord."

Who are we to tell God what must be? "For as the heavens are higher than the earth, so are my ways higher than your ways, and my thoughts higher than your thoughts."

Jesus calls us from worries about the future. "Follow me," he says. And so I shall! As the old hymn says,

> In thee is gladness
> Amid all sadness,
> Jesus, sunshine of my heart!

> *—Johann Lindemann*

With such a harvest of faith, I can go on living day by day.

> My life is a book, an open book,
> Made known to all through the years.
> Each chapter's engraved on this heart of mine,
> And each day a new page appears.

> *—Unknown*

Each day is like a furrow lying before us. Our thoughts, desires, and actions are the seeds that each minute we drop into the earth, without much awareness. One furrow finished, we commence another, then another, and yet another. Each day presents a fresh furrow, and so on to the end of life, sowing, ever sowing.

All we have sown springs up, grows, and bears fruit almost unknown to us. Even if by chance we cast a backward glance, we often fail to recognize our work and cannot tally up the harvest. Behind us, angels and demons, like gleaners, gather in sheaves all that belongs to them. Every night their store is increased. They preserve it, and at the last day will present it to their master (*Gold Dust*).

O Lord, if I have been sowing seeds of selfishness, unkindness, sinfulness, let me diligently and carefully weed out what has sprung up. In their place, let me sow seeds of goodness and righteousness.

In the time I have left with my family, help me to be kind and true! How sharply aware you have made me just now that we have such a little way to go together. Let us cherish and treasure each friendship while we have the chance.

So soon it will be time to say farewell. May we all meet again some day on that celestial shore, where parting hands are known no more. ❧

Scripture References

YEAR TWELVE
July 31: 1 Tim. 4:8
Aug. 7: Exod. 20:4
Aug. 8: 1 Cor. 8:13
Oct. 3: Mark 10:18
Oct. 31: Matt. 5:44
Nov. 11: 2 Sam. 11–12
Dec. 17: Rom. 12:17-21

YEAR THIRTEEN
Jan. 8: Col. 3:12
Jan. 22: 1 Pet. 2:9; 1 John 4:19
Jan. 28: Mark 16:15; 8:34
Feb. 2: Jer. 8:22
Feb. 11: Matt. 10:28
Feb. 14: Matt. 7:1-5
Feb. 17: Phil. 4:8; Prov. 31:27; Luke 1:38; John 11
Mar. 9: Prov. 16:18-19
Mar. 25: Ps. 30:5
May 15: Song of Sol. 2:12
May 19: Lev. 19:18; Matt. 19:19; 22:39; Mark 12:31; Luke 10:29; Rom. 13:9; Gal. 5:14; James 2:8
June 18: Ps. 104:24
July 2: Isa. 43:2
July 3: Job 13:15; 1:21; Isa. 55:9; Matt. 6:25-34; John 21:22; Acts 1:7

Other Credits

"Thankfulness for What You Could Not Afford" is used by permission from the periodical *Missionary Messenger*, Memphis, Tenn. The poem "The Unbarred Door," by an unknown author, is from *Seeking True Values*, excerpted and summarized by permission of Pathway Publishers, Aylmer, Ont. The story "Such a Little Way Together," by Herman W. Gockel, is from *My Hand in His*, used by permission of Concordia Publishing House, St. Louis, Mo. *Now Is the Time to Love,* by John M. Drescher, was published by Herald Press in 1970. The furrow parable is adapted from *Gold Dust*, translated from *Paillettes d'or*. Poets are identified in the text for poems briefly quoted or from more than a century ago.

The Author

The author's pen name is Carrie Bender. She is a member of an old order group. With her husband and children, she lives among the Amish in Lancaster County, Pennsylvania.